M000026035

The Land of Amer

Nauman A. Raja

Copyright © 2019 Nauman A. Raja
All rights reserved.
ISBN: 9781976716904

ACKNOWLEDGMENTS

A warm and special thank you to my dear friends, Amina and Maria, for the lovely artwork that accompanies my story.

Thank you forever!

THE LAND OF AMER: a map

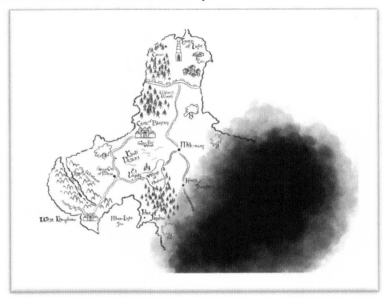

About this book

Since the Golden Age, the Land of Amer has been driven by a cycle of light and dark, life and death.

The light is slowly draining away from the lands of the Amer, but in the North Kingdom, the land is untouched. The inhabitants there are unfazed by the dark, because they live in the safety of the Golden Gates and the brilliance that emanates from the Tower of Light, which blesses them with everlasting life. Only a few in the North will not stand for the injustice the darkness bestows—and yet, even then, they know not what the dark clouds truly bring: a curse...a curse, not in the mind, but in the heart.

CONTENTS

PROLOGUE

Since the fall of the Golden Age, the Land of Amer knew only light and dark, life and death. The sky blackened. Darkness grew beyond all the Middle-lands.

War brought bloodshed, and the Norm villagers from the Middle-lands fled to the north. They begged for days at the Golden Gates of the north until the watchers finally opened the gates to them.

Among them was a young boy who lost his family in the massive slaughter at Mik-Mag. He spoke about the Jinns—dark-armored soldiers riding on large spiders. They cursed anyone who laid eyes on them.

He had survived the attack, but nightmares plagued his sleep and grief ruled his days.

The young Norm was taken to the Tower of Light to tell his tale to King Alm. The young king heard the Norm's story of the darkness that was growing in the Middle-lands and the war that it was bringing.

"Some say the darkness moves north," King Alm told the boy. "This is why I ask you about these horrors."

"Will you help us?" The boy lifted his head, searching King Alm's face. There was no deception there, only clear confidence and bright courage. King Alm's voice was as powerful as his countenance.

"Yes."

Within a few months, King Alm marched at the head of his army to the Middle-lands.

It was the first time the Norms had seen the power of the north and fury of the Golden Soldiers. They were awed by the golden blades, the golden armor and the bravery of the soldiers.

Their hope grew when Lovnor, the young prince of the Qazams, led his elven army to join the Golden Soldiers and battle alongside them.

They fought all injustices they came across, but the war was fierce and long. Months of fighting turned into years of despair as the Golden Soldiers and the Qazam armies battled with different tribes of the Middle-lands.

The foes only wore black charred armor, and as the young boy had witnessed, they rode on enormous spiders. They seemed undefeatable. They brought fear and death as they spread across the Middle-lands. Ubir followed them, feeding on the living or the dead.

"I promised I would help the Norms," King Alm told Prince Lovnor, as they leaned over a battle map, planning their next strategy. Weariness edged his voice, and his young face now held the hardness of grief and fear.

"This darkness is a curse," Prince Lovnor said. "It is not just bloodshed and conflict. It is a shadow that spreads into the hearts of our men. They are losing their compassion, and they begin to despair."

"It was the sight at Mik-Mag," King Alm said. He closed his eyes. "The lands were burned and barren. Mothers held scorched babies, fathers ran in fear, and all the children lay dead. No wonder they fled from us."

For a long moment, the battle tent fell silent. King Alm leaned forward onto the table, studying the map in front of him. He jabbed his finger at the right side of the parchment.

"Some people say that a great evil is brewing in the far east," he said. "We need more men."

That evening, he sent a raven to the Land of Sea and Mountains in the west, requesting aid. The old king of the West-lands sent ten thousand of his strongest knights to aid in King Alm's holy crusade. Marching with a mixture of Qazams, Norms, and Westerns, the young king led his army on his massive talking lion, Amir.

When the army reached the Lands of the East, they saw nothing but darkness and black clouds. Lightning strikes brought barely enough light for them to see their surroundings. Dead bodies of men and women from the Middle-lands littered the ground with every step they took.

"Stop." King Alm held up a hand, halting his armies as Amir froze mid-step.

In the distance stood a massive dark shadow with glowing red eyes of fire.

Prince Umar

CHAPTER ONE –
The Call of the North

The wind blew, gusting and huffing through the sand. Above its mournful whistles, the clanking sounds of metal on metal grew louder. The Golden Gates of the north groaned as they parted, swinging wide open for the second time in the Land of Amer's history.

The radiant bright light of the north crept beneath the gate doors as it opened, illuminating the lands beyond it. Horns blew. Horses marched forward, and golden chains of armor clashed as young soldiers, many of them in their late teens, moved forward resolutely.

No elders rode in this cavalry. These young men replaced their forefathers, who had gone with King Alm on his first crusade. It was a testament to the years that had passed. The young soldiers of the North aged more slowly than their Norm friends, but each teen among them was as old as a Norm elder.

Their golden chest pieces were engraved with a mighty white lion paw. Some of the other pieces of armor were ill-fitting for a few of the soldiers, whose attire had been handed down from their forefathers.

Most of the soldiers had long, dark, straight, black hair that never moved, even when the horses pranced forward. Their eyes were mostly green, although a few soldiers had brown eyes. Fewer still had eyes of bright white, indicating the kin of the High King. Unlike the Qazams, the elves of the western woods, all of the soldiers had light brown skin like the Norms of the West-lands.

Prince Umar, the eldest son of King Alm, marched his horse forward to the gates, leading the armies behind him. He raised a fist in the air, shouting the High King's favorite chant. "We fear nothing but the Lord! We will fight and defeat anything that endangers our kingdom!

The tall Golden Gates, which had never been attacked or overturned, towered above Prince Umar. He appraised their height as he rode threw them.

Far above, the watchers peered down at the army through their thick blindfolds, as if they could see them instead of simply sensing their presence. These watchers always stayed at the top of the

Golden Gates, sitting in complete stillness most of the time as they used their minds and emotions to feel for darkness or danger coming from the Middle-lands. The colors of their blindfolds showed their ranks. Elder watchers covered their eyes with black cloth. The novices, who trained with these elders, wore lighter blindfolds of white, gray or blue.

Prince Umar knew the cycle of duty never ended. The younger watchers lost their sight, but they learned from the elder watchers how to feel the shape of the darkness, the way the Golden Gates connected the two seas that lapped the shores on either side of it, and the edge of the wall, which towered 800 feet above the path he now rode. In the far distance, he could just make out the homes of the elder watchers, which were made of wood from the High King's forest. They had triangular roofs that were barely illuminated by a faint ray of light from the Tower of Light.

An elder watcher from the top of the golden wall yelled down, catching Prince Umar's eyes.

"Young prince, how long will the army stay in the dark lands beyond the gates?"

"Three moon passes, and then we shall return," Prince Umar replied. His deep voice was as rich as the three beautiful green gems that he wore on his armor and the long, gold-trimmed cape. His black hair hung free around his face.

The elder watcher tilted his head, almost as if he glanced at the jewels, and Prince Umar smiled. "Some say I shouldn't wear these gems to battle, because it shows a sign of pride," he said, "But I want

3

my men to have faith in me. They need to see me unafraid of losing or dying."

The elder watcher nodded and waved Prince Umar through the gates. The mission of the convoy was simple: reach the Middle-lands and fight back anyone who might bring harm to these lands of Amer.

Even so, the devastation from the first crusades had crushed the spirits of many men. Prince Umar looked over his shoulder as his army marched past the arched gates. Their long dark hair came into view, and their faces held determination and honor. Their fates were sealed. Whether they lived or died, they intended to complete the High King's mission.

Among them, Prince Umar's younger brothers, Prince Kaf and Prince Adn, rode side by side. Prince Umar watched as his brothers whispered. His heart ached. They sat firmly on top of their horses, not knowing what was to come, but their faces shone with hope and excitement. In spite of the near-certainty of upcoming battles, they were happy to finally see what adventures the south land held.

Young Prince Kaf laughed as he waved at Prince Umar, and then turned to his other brother. "Are you ready?"

"I hope I am, but I can never be too sure," Prince Adn replied. "We've never seen the lands beyond the gates before. O-Father says only mischief lies in the south, and he's still sad about what happened in the east, in the Land of the Unknown. He wears that grief on his face every day."

"I have been eagerly awaiting this day," Prince Kaf said. "I've been looking forward to it ever since our O-Father told us that we'll be marching to the Middle-lands."

Prince Adn glanced at Prince Kaf, and his eyebrows rose slightly. He might have said something in return, but Prince Kaf spoke again, looking deep into the dark lands of the south as his voice grew low and serious.

"Staying inside the Tower of Light was like living in a prison," he said, "And I hated constantly training when we stayed at the cabin in the King's Forest with Uncle Adu. Now I feel purpose behind all the hard work. Something out there is calling me." He nodded at the dark lands ahead, choked with a sudden emotion that ran deeper than excitement.

"I know what you mean, but this is not a game anymore," Adn said. "Remember, we must listen to Umar. You can't run off on a whim, like you used to during training." He looked straight into Kaf's eyes, but they were filled with inner thoughts. Adn sighed. "You're not paying any attention to me, are you?"

Kaf replied with two words. "Za-Labit, march!" The young princes' personal bodyguard galloped to the front of the Golden Army.

Immediately outside the gates, the ground was pummeled by the hooves of cavalry horses and foot soldiers. The light faded as they marched forward. Behind them, the Golden Gates began to close, and the bright lands beyond them grew dimmer, disappearing when the gates thudded shut.

The elder gate watcher yelled from the top of the wall once more. "See you in three moon passes." A few of the soldiers looked up at the watchers, nodding their hope and determination, and Prince Umar waved at them once more.

"It's hard to see them go." A young watcher named Jud sat down beside the elder watcher. "Jamil, we haven't opened these gates in many years." He felt the Golden Army marching forward toward the nearest village. They held their banners high. Someone started singing, and it seemed as if the entire army joined in the anthem. Chills ran down Jud's arms, and he spoke again.

"Many of those soldiers are my friends and my kin," he said. "I do not know if I will see them again."

"Yes," Jamil replied, "But the darkness is growing, and it's changing into something I've never felt before. The last time I felt anything similar was when High King Alm was young."

"That must have been in the Golden Age," Jud said. "I heard he marched into the Middle-lands on his great lion, Amir."

Jamil nodded, and his lined face grew bleak. "The High King hasn't been the same since the battle in the Lands of the Unknown," he said.

Jud turned, grabbed Jamil's hands and tugged, helping the fragile elder watcher stand. As the army faded into the distance, Jamil leaned on Jud as they slowly walked back to his tent.

"How many soldiers marched in the past?" Jud asked.

"Many." Jamil swallowed before speaking again. "In those days, the Norms and Qazams were united with the Northern Kin. They marched in the thousands as far as the eye could see. I was young then. I had not taken the oath yet, so I didn't have

6

the cloth, but I wish I had been able to go with them."

"Why? Why would you want to wear the cloth while you were too young to do so?" Jud's voice filled with shock, and Jamil's words filled with emotion.

"I watched my friends leave and return, just as you watched your friends leave today. Only a few of my kin who left returned, and when they did, their white clothing was covered in blood. None of them ever spoke about what happened in the east land, so I do not know what happened there."

"You felt it, though," Jud said.

"No," Jamil said. "I felt evil, but I did not know what happened, nor do I want to find out, if that darkness comes here."

Jud held the tent flap open, helped Jamil step inside, and walked him to a narrow bed. Jamil grabbed the side of it and sank down heavily. He lay down carefully, as if he needed time to measure his next words.

"Jud, remember who we are," he said. "I know watching your friends leave is hard on you, and it was on me too, but do not lose hope. We still have our Tower of Light." He pointed to a desk laden with ink, paper, and quills. "We must send a seal to the High King."

The Tower of Light

CHAPTER TWO –
The Tower of Light

Ravens flew over the North. Below them, a land of pure nature and thick-scented green landscape filled with the sounds of running water, chirping birds and a permeating sense of joy. In the distance, the Tower of Light stood as a beacon, the source of light that allowed nature to spread far throughout the northern lands.

Some said the Golden Gates restricted the light, holding the full power back from spreading into the Middle-lands. What lay beyond the Tower of

Light was unknown to anyone except High King Alm, but the light from the tower had special powers that gave the king and his kin long, everlasting life.

The ravens flapped their wings, casting blurred shadows where the King's Road split into three paths.

One fork of the path led to the far west, where the Qazams built tree homes in thick forests. There, the air was always full of the comforting scent of wood. The Qazams had lived in those lands since the Golden Age. Only High King Alm knew their origin, but he never spoke of it. The king of the Qazams always stayed in his own lands.

The right fork of the King's Road led to the home of the Norms. These people were those from the Middle-lands, the descendants of those that High King Alm had allowed to pass through northward through the Golden Gates when the darkness first arose. The Norms aged quickly, and they were always building and digging to find gold. Qazams and the kin of the North found them odd, but they were the first to rise to the aid of High King Alm. In his lands, they lived in peace, and their numbers grew large.

The center path, where the King's Road split, was the only way to the Kingdom of the North, where High King Alm lived.

As the ravens reached the Tower of Light, soft white snow fell slowly and melted in the bright light. In the west, songs of this snow's beauty were sung, but only a few ever saw the beauty of the continuously falling and melting snow.

This was the silver age. Tough times had hardened the heart of the Hight King. The darkness grew, and he felt it.

The ravens reached their aviary in the Tower of Light. A soldier appeared, retrieved the message that the watchers had sent, and carried the sealed note down through the castle. Notes such as these were always meant for Zubair.

Zubair was the High King's most skilled fighter and the High King's right-hand man. He had never lost a battle, and so the High King gave him a title, the "Order of Abdulaziz." In all the northern lands, only Zubair bore this title.

"My Afand. Sir. A seal has come from the watchers on the Golden Gates," the soldier said. He handed the sealed note to Zubair.

"Shukran. Thank you. I'll deliver this to the High King immediately," Zubair replied.

Zubair made his way toward the throne room. Inside, the king sat on a tall throne made of two golden chairs. One of the chairs was empty. Behind the throne, enormous glass windows looked over the land below, and a glowing bright light slowly crept against the walls. Zubair bowed as he approached the throne.

"My High King, we have received a seal stating the young princes have passed the arch and are now heading to the Middle-lands," Zubair said.

"Good." King Alm blinked, as if Zubair had shaken him out of deep thoughts. "Troubled times are coming," he said. "We need to act fast, and we need more riders to be sent to this fight. Our armies are too small in number."

The High King stood and stepped slowly down the dais. "This will not be easy," he said. He sighed, and his lion, Amir, looked up immediately, preparing for action.

"Yes, my High King," Zubair said. "I'll send seals to the tribes of the Norms. I will inform them of our need for riders to be sent to the Middle-lands."

"And send a seal to the Qazams," the High King added. He looked almost eager. Zubair nodded his head in agreement and walked away.

The throne room was empty again. The High King stared for a moment at the empty chair where his queen once sat, overwhelmed by emotions. He needed air.

On a balcony overlooking the Land of Amer, King Alm took in the gradually falling snow, the sea-like blue sky, and the sounds of songbirds in the trees below. In the distance, the Tower of Light glistened with rays of golden light that reflected on every river and pond.

It was beautiful, but it was the last thing in the High King's mind. He remembered Golden Age, and the first days when he marched south with his army past the Golden Gates. He had been so full of hope. He reflected on all the battles that he fought in the dark lands, and he grieved for all the soldiers who lost their souls.

These horrors had changed the High King, and he knew it.

"I am no king," he said, and Amir padded softly to his side as he spoke. "I am not fit to be a leader. I was unaware of my own blindness when I was young, and I was unaware of this darkness, this great curse. It spreads even in my own heart." Sorrow filled all the lines in his face, and as the memories of what happened in the Land of the Unknown resurfaced, his heart flooded with darkness.

"I never thought the day would come when our gates would open again," Amir said.

Amir's deep growling voice broke the High King's reverie, and he laughed. "Do not worry. We did not send your kin, Lion Amir."

"Thank the Lord. I don't want them to see the Middle-lands again." Amir sighed, and they both laughed. A raven flew in the sky again, bending toward the land of the Norms with a sealed note attached to its leg.

Qazam King Idun

CHAPTER THREE –
Call to Arms

A raven carried another sealed note from the High King into the woods of the Qazams, who built their houses in the trees. Unlike the Norms, the Qazams never cut down trees or plants, so the peaceful forest land was laced with tree roots and high bushes. For most of the Qazams who lived there, it was a place of deep spirituality.

As the raven flew further into the forest, the bright blue lights hanging from the trees illuminated the marble stones of the Qazam homes. On the forest floor, young Qazams trained with bows and wooden swords. Their ankle-length red clothes and long blonde hair flowed as they moved. They jumped over streams and dodged between the trees, where afternoon sunlight split into rays of golden warmth.

The raven passed the pillars of the king's palace, circling once above the statue of a stately king. King Idun was a fair king who never left his home. Grief over the loss of his eldest son, Lovnor, in the Lands of the Unknown, still haunted him.

A young Qazam looked up as the raven settled on the balcony outside the throne room. He stood, twitching his long, pointy ears, and retrieved the note tied to the raven's leg.

"King Idun, a seal has come from High King Alm," he said.

"What does the seal say?" King Idun, who had been reading a document, now held his hand in the air. The young Qazam opened the seal, and his face paled. He spoke slowly, nervously, hoping not to anger his king.

"My Old Friend Idun, I haven't sent you a seal in many moon passes, but another time of darkness has come. We need your aid. Send your Qazam warriors to fight with Prince Umar. Together we can cleanse the Land of Amer."

King Idun's face hardened, and his hands tightened into fists, crumpling the document he still held. His voice thundered.

"He wants what? How dare the High King ask for our aid again!"

King Idun's eyes zipped around the room, searching for an outlet for his anger.

"I'm sorry, my king!" The young Qazam leapt back, just in time for his father to grab him and shove him out of the throne room.

"Don't come back until he calms down," his father hissed. The young Qazam fled, and his father reluctantly turned back into the throne room. No one wanted to face King Idun's anger.

The king stood, biting the inside of his cheeks, but he was straightening out and smoothing the document he had nearly destroyed. His long, red cape swung low around his thin feet. The golden crown he wore tilted on his head, and one of the decorative thorns it bore threatened to scratch his forehead. Even then, his long blonde hair appeared to have not moved at all.

"My apologies for my son," the other man said, bowing low.

"Don't worry about it." King Idun set the document resolutely on a side table and turned to face his servant, but a vein still pulsed in the side of his neck. "I lost my temper, but I am not angry at your son. My anger is for our High King, who wants our people to spill their blood again, and for what? For some Norms living in the Middle-lands, whom we have never seen."

He puffed his cheeks out and took an enormous breath, but before he could speak again, a beautiful, delicate voice spoke King Idun's name. The light dimmed slightly. Idun and his servant paused and turned as Queen Meltôriel approached.

"What is troubling you, my love?" Heaven's light shone in Meltôriel's eyes as she searched her husband's face, and he replied more sharply than he meant to.

"Nothing that may worry you, my Queen."

She almost smiled. Instead, she glanced at the servant man, who had been glancing over his shoulder as if to make certain his son was safe. She caught his eye and nodded once. Relief washed over his face. He nodded in return, bowed to the king, and left.

"Now tell me what's troubling you," Meltôriel said.

"King Alm wants war. The last time we aided him, our eldest son died, just for the Norms who live in the Middle-lands."

King Idun's face darkened, and he closed his eyes, squeezing them tight. His breath came in ragged bursts. "It's too much," he said, wiping a hand across his face. "All these decades later, the pain is too much. I relive his loss every day."

Meltôriel reached for Idun's pale hands and studied the blue veins showing through the skin for some time before she raised her head again. When she spoke, she looked directly into Idun's green eyes.

"The High King lost something, too, that day," she said. "We cannot undo what was done in the Land of the Unknown, but we can move forward from that moment now."

Neither of them noticed the servant man enter, release the raven and leave again, or the pale face of his son peering fearfully into the throne room. Idun swallowed a sob, pulled Meltôriel close and held her. The raven flapped its wings and took silently to the air.

Norms of the North

CHAPTER FOUR –
Iron and Fury

Yet another raven flew east, nearly parallel to the great wall. The raven's shadow brushed the back of a horse running freely in an open field of green grass. On the outskirts of a Norm village below the raven's flight, young children ran and played. Their laughter echoed in the birdsongs.

To the north, an amazing array of light caught the raven's eye. The Tower of Light could still be seen in the distance, but here, in this place, the Norms lived.

Norms, or the Normal people of the Land of Amer, were the designated builders of the North.

They maintained the buildings, the roads, the walkways and had even aided the High King when he built the Tower of Light itself. They were masters in the crafts of woodworking, weaponry, masonry and especially, making steel. They were also the first race to discover and use gold.

The metalwork set the Norms aside from the other Northern Kin more than anything else. They supplied all the metal items, from weapons to plates. In return, the High King gave them ivory gems.

As the raven flew into the stone castle, large numbers of Norms in the courtyard below worked on several different projects. Steel was melting in an enormous, open-roofed blacksmith shop with a massive fire in its center. Hammers clashed with steel. Norms yelled at each other over the noise, and black dust hung heavy in the air.

The raven spun, avoiding a cloud of smoke. Below it, a group of Norms were creating swords and armor with heavy melted iron.

"When can we have a break?"

Danish, a young norm learning the blacksmithing trade, spoke up breathlessly. His face was red from the heat, and sweat dripped from his hair across his forehead.

"This is the third break you asked for. Carry on with your work, you ass-clown!" Blaize, the teacher, didn't have much patience for the young learners.

"I can't learn when I'm hungry," Danish said. He smiled as if he hoped it would get him on Blaize's good side.

It worked.

"Fine, but only 5 minutes," said Blaize. Danish and a handful of other students ran out of the castle, away from the thick black dust and into the fresh air beyond the smithies.

"Great hall! Great hall!" A soldier called out to all of the workers in the courtyard.

"Again?" Blaize glanced at his fellow workers. They appeared as annoyed as he felt. They walked from the courtyard into the castle and climbed the stairs to the great hall.

As he entered, he saw the Norm king already seated at the far end of the room. It was a cramped space, with tables set end to end and drinks on most of them.

The Norms pushed and shoved their way into the room until they sat in every available space. They chattered, and some drank, and the noise rose to a din.

"Shut it!" King Duncan stood, holding the seal that the raven had now delivered. The noise stopped abruptly.

"Many of you know that the Golden Gates were opened, and the young princes are marching into the Middle-lands," he said.

Murmurs rose again as the Norms whispered to each other, wondering why.

One Norm rose his hand and hollered over the rising chatter. "What does the seal say?"

King Duncan moved into the middle of the great hall, reading the seal to his people as he paced in one of the only empty spots in the room.

"Your Father aided me in the war at the end of the Golden Age, and I ask again for the Norms to aid us. We need to fightback against the darkness, because it is growing. Send your riders to aid my eldest son, Prince Umar, in the city of Mik-Mag."

"The High King wants another war," Blaize said. "Does he remember last time we went to war?"

He looked around the room. Danish and the other innocent children had been rounded up and were now listening, sitting on the floor just a few feet from where he stood. They blinked, unable to comprehend the idea of war, while the room buzzed with conversation again. Most of the voices disagreed with the High King's request for aid.

King Duncan silenced them again. He pointed to the flag hanging from the rafters above them.

"Do you see my father's face?" He nodded at the center of the flag, where the image of King Dyfed peered down at the crowd. "I would rather die than dishonor my father."

King Duncan folded the seal and slipped it inside his brocaded belt. He glanced around the room, catching the eyes of as many Norms as he could, and his voice grew bold.

"We were given this land by King Alm. His people protected us and kept us away from what we all came from," he said. "A few of you might remember the bloodshed we had in the city of Mik-Mag during the end of the Golden Age. Women and men fled like animals, leaving everything behind. Some even left their children."

He turned, facing the other side of the room, and stretched out his hands, appealing to the crowd. "Now that we have peace, shall we turn our backs on those who are our kin who still live in those lands?"

His eyes blazed with the passion of honor, and although his face was serious, his voice held the confidence of an entire nation. "No. I shall not let us forget. We will ride to the Golden Gates, and then we will ride south to join the princes and aid them in this war."

King Duncan raised his fist into the air. "We are the Norms of the North. We are full of iron and fury. We will fight like wild animals and show no mercy to those who took the lives of our kin so many years ago. life many years ago! Who will follow me? Who will help me avenge our kin and bring peace to their souls?"

The faces of the Norms around him lit up, as if he had kindled fire in their hearts. It shone in their eyes, which were riveted on his form as he spoke again.

"If I am truly your king, then follow me!"

A cheer rose from somewhere in the room, and other Norms joined until all were standing, clapping and shouting. King Duncan signed an agreement to aid King Alm in his new holy crusade, and a new round of cheers rose inside the great hall.

On the far side of the room, Blaize rubbed his chin thoughtfully. He wasn't the only one to disapprove of this decision, but he was outnumbered. He watched as King Duncan called two captains to his side.

"My King, we'll start preparing now," one of the captains said.

"Good. We also need to send a seal to the raiders near the High King's forest. They do not know what happened here today, but if they think they can stay in the North without fighting for our cause, they have something else coming to them."

King Duncan's forehead furrowed, as if he sensed they might not be as easy to persuade as the Norms in nearer the castle.

"My King, those Norm will not fight with us," the captain said. "They are raiders, and their lives are built on different principles. If they do come, they will kill us after we leave the Golden Gates. Let's leave them alone, or kill them before they can kill us."

The king wasn't moved.

"If you do not send seals, I'll ask you to ride up to the raiders personally and make a request for their fighters to join us. The choice is ours, but I want this done!"

King Duncan walked away, and the captains looked at each other. Concern filled their faces. Blaize noted it and turned on his heel, following King Duncan as he exited the great hall.

"My king, why are we doing this?" Blaize called. "We live in time of peace!"

He glanced down, just now realizing that Danish had slipped his tiny hand into Blaize's large, work-roughened one. Danish looked scared.

King Duncan stopped and turned. When he saw the look on the young boy's face, he lifted Danish' chin with one of his fingers.

"Don't be worried, young child. None shall fear while the Tower of Light still glows," he said. He bent down and placed his hand on Danish's shoulder. "Tell me, who is your father?"

"My father is Margrethe," Danish said. His voice shook. King Duncan took a step back.

"Oh," the king said. "Margrethe, the warrior who was lost during the first great war?"

King Duncan smiled, trying to cover the shock this news had given him.

"Your father was a great man, always willing to fight a great battle," King Duncan said. He placed a gold coin in Blaize's hand. "Take this young child and buy him the finest armor."

Danish blinked at the brilliance of the gold. While he was distracted, King Duncan leaned close to Blaize and whispered.

"You come with me to the south."

The king walked quickly away, before either Blaize or Danish could regain their composure.

The next few weeks were even busier. The fires in the smithies never died, and the Norms built faster than ever. A few began to pack for the battle.

"I never thought this day would come," most of the younger Norms said, when they spoke among themselves. "I never thought this would be our fate."

Blaize overheard them many times, but no one dared stand up to King Duncan. They would die for their insolence to him. If they didn't stand up to him, they faced possible death in battle, instead.

CHAPTER FIVE – Unpleasant Weather

Rain fell continuously, and the temperature dropped. As the army moved, the grass around them slowly lost its color, and the clouds turned shady and black. They completely blocked the sun, which was something the Golden Army had never seen before.

For many of the young soldiers, this was a time of excitement and celebration. No matter how dark the skies grew, this was the first time they had ever been away from their elders.

"Wow, I've never had this much freedom," one boy said. "We can do whatever we want. We don't have to train, there's no clean-up and best of all, there's no bed-time, but I'll miss going to prayer and giving my respect."

"I know, nobody is here to tell us what to do and how to do it. We just need to get to the city of Mik-Mag...I bet they would love to have us there," another boy said as he laughed.

The Golden Army marched south twice as slowly as they normally would because soldiers often broke ranks to run and play. Mik-Mag was only two days ride from the Golden Gates, but at this slow pace, the army wouldn't reach it until the evening of the fourth day. The army wasn't as disciplined as Prince Umar hoped.

He glanced behind him, frowning at a group of soldiers who had dismounted and were running around. Behind them and around them, other soldiers rode in poor form and out of the single-file line he had designated for them.

"ZA- tawa!" Umar yelled, and the army stopped abruptly. The jokes and laughter faded away as he stepped off his horse, dragging his cape through the dirt as he stepped quickly toward the disobedient group of soldiers. His eyes held fire and fury, and his boots pounded the ground.

"Listen closely because I'm not repeating myself again," he said. "We are on a mission. We are not here for fun or for pleasure. There will be no more jumping off your horses, and no more running around, because we'll never make it to the city of Mik-Mag at this rate."

Prince Umar took a deep breath and stared into the eyes of his men. "I understand some of you are young and eager to be away from home," he said. "I know it's nice to be free, to not take orders from the elders or from Adu, but let's get to the city. Once we're there, we can have a break and kick back," he said.

"Why can't we stop here and have a break now?" One boy asked, as he reached for the reins of his horse. "We've been riding for a while now."

A few others nodded.

"I agree. We're all tired," said another young soldier.

"Are you saying that you did not take your riding lessons from Adu?" replied Umar. "You know he always said to stay on the horse as long as possible."

"Adu always said taking breaks helps the soul," the insolent youth said, and Prince Umar had to hide a smile behind his hand.

"He totally did." Prince Umar chuckled, looked around at his men, and smiled openly. He stepped up beside the boy, who had just mounted his horse again, and pulled him off.

"Let's take that break now after all, huh?" said Umar. His soldiers and kin cheered and dismounted, ready to relax even under the dark skies.

"I really should take it easy on them," Prince Umar said to himself. "They're only children, only maybe 35 years in Norm age."

The young kin of the Golden Army played tag and held races on the flat land around them. There were no other people here, no houses, and no travelers. Sometimes, though, they stepped on what they thought were rocks and found them to be small white bones.

One boy picked up a bone in his hands and held it out to a friend. "What do you think this could be?" he asked.

"It's too small to be a Norm bone," said another boy. "I think it must be the bone of an animal that used to live around here."

"My father used to tell us stories about when he was a boy, and he came to the city of Mik-Mag," another soldier said. "They found almost no animals. Those that they did find were slowly dying."

Adn, who had been watching this group of soldiers, stepped up to take a closer look at the bone.

"Let's hope we don't continue seeing these," he said. "This is scary. In the north, Norms always took care of their wildlife. These animals must have died because they had no food to eat and or they were hunted to death."

The rain and dark clouds swelling up in the south were getting to Prince Kaf. Racing around on a field of bones was spooky, no matter how much fun the younger soldiers thought it was. Kaf turned away from Adn and went to find Prince Umar. He tried to hide his worry, but it leaked through his voice anyway.

"Brother Umar, why have we stopped?" he asked.

"There's nothing to worry about," Prince Umar said. "We just stopped to take a quick break and let the young ones have a little fun. I think Adu would have done the same, right?"

Prince Umar kept a straight face the entire time he looked at Kaf, but his shoulders shook, and Kaf knew Umar was struggling to hold in his laughter.

"You wish Adu would have let us take a break," Adn said, coming up behind them. Kaf and Umar burst into laughter.

"He would have beaten us even thinking of the words 'taking a break'," Umar said.

Kaf's laughter died quickly. "I'm not tired, nor do I need to take a break," he said. "This place gives me the creeps. Would it be okay if I and a few soldiers ride up ahead? I'd like to get to the city as soon as we can."

Even though he stopped speaking, his eyes held the plea of his thoughts. He wanted Prince Umar to say yes.

Umar glanced at the troops and then back at Kaf. "It doesn't seem right to indulge the soldiers and not indulge you, too," he said, and his own laughter faded away. "Promise not to do anything that would make me mad, and I think that riding ahead would be okay."

Kaf smiled. His sense of eagerness had returned.

"Of course, my habibi," he said. "We'll wait for you at the city of Mik-Mag."

Within a few short minutes, Kaf had gathered a group of soldiers to ride ahead with him. He nodded at his brothers and rode forward, disappearing under the thick clouds that now rolled with thunder.

A sense of discomfort and anxiety replaced Prince Umar's light-hearted compassion. He called the playing soldiers back to their horses, reprimanded some of them for moving too slowly, and got the army moving forward again. As they followed in Kaf's wake, Prince Umar had only one thought. He looked forward, searching the horizon where Kaf and his men had disappeared.

"May God keep you safe," he whispered.

CHAPTER SIX –
Bitter Farewell, Part 1

King Idun walked into the fine Qazam garden, appreciating the birds he saw flying in the distance and the amazing sunbeams dancing in the sky. This time of day was the highlight of every day, not just because of the beauty of the forest, but because King Idun had the chance to watch his youngest son's education.

Prince Sumer was agile, but the elders teaching him spoke in a harshness meant to motivate him even more.

"Faster! You can't beat a norm with those speeds," said an elder Qazam to Sumer, who was running past a line of practice dummies. Their heads had been adorned with a likeness of the late King Dyfed. "Release the arrows!" the elder yelled, and the zip and twang of bowstrings and arrows taking flight almost broke Sumer's concentration.

Sumer was small for a Qazam, but he was fast on his feet. He leapt in the air with two arrows in his left hand, nocked them, and aimed. One arrow sank deep into a dummy head, and the other sliced through a leaf behind the Elder Qazam.

"Sumer!" King Idun yelled. "Over here, now!"

"I'm sorry, father," Sumer said. "I did not know you were here."

"I saw what you did," Idun said. "Do not show disrespect to your elders, even by aiming at a target near them. You still have a lot to learn. Do not get ahead of yourself so early on."

"Yes, father." Sumer looked a little sullen, but King Idun's next words cheered him again.

"I'm only telling you these things because I have big things in store for you," Idun said. "I hope this first mission I have for you will make you a stronger leader."

"What mission, Father?" Sumer tried to catch his father's eyes as they walked together out of the garden. They passed the statue of Idun and walked through the courtyard of fine green grass before King Idun spoke again.

"I have a task for you," Idun said finally, and his face was as hard as the marble walls around them. "This is a most difficult thing for me to ask. The last time I assigned this task..."

His voice broke, and he turned away. Sumer looked so much like Lovnor that he couldn't face him and give him the same task he had given his eldest son.

"What do you need me to do, Father?" Sumer's voice was gentle, but eager, too. King Idun was an indulgent father, but that meant finding ways to truly impress him were hard to come by.

"A Seal has come from the High King, and they need aid in the south of the Golden Gates," King Idun said. He began to speak again, but Sumer was already replying.

"Yes," he said, nodding his head firmly. "Yes. This was once Lovnor's task. I am honored to follow in his footsteps."

Idun looked at his last son. He blinked hard, fighting tears that he didn't want his son to see. "You have courage," he said. "You will need that."

They entered the great hall together, where music and the sound of laughter filled the air. Like the soldiers from Prince Umar's army, the young Qazam soldiers in the hall were eager to march south of the Golden Gates.

"There's no point in training, if you're not willing to fight, huh lads?" said a beautiful young Qazam woman.

"Yes, Aysha!" The young soldiers answered her happily, but she only looked at Sumer, as if she hoped he would notice her.

"Enough cheering," King Idun told the soldiers. "Gear up and meet in the honor room." He patted Sumer on the shoulders and walked away. His long red cape swirled behind his ankles.

Aysha moved close to Sumer. "Did you tell him? "she asked.

Sumer blushed and grew shy. "No," he said. He gazed at Aysha, but she was already walking away to get ready.

"But you will, right?" she said over her shoulder as she stepped into the honor room.

The honor room was full of Qazam history. There was an enormous picture of Qazams crossing what they called the low river. Blessed swords and shields hung on the walls, reflected in the polished white stones of the floor. A thick book full of legacy stories lay open on a great wooden table at the head of the hall, near King Idun's throne.

As the soldiers filed in, they sat on either side of the hall at gigantic wooden tables and chairs carved from the roots of trees that had died in the forest.

King Idun walked arrogantly toward his throne and sat forward on it, raising his hands in the air.

"As many of you know, the Lion Amir had a vison of great danger brewing in the midlands. Now a raven has come from the High King, requesting our aid. His eldest son, Umar, has already led an army past the Golden Gates. They are heading to the city Mik-Mag. Sumer will lead you, and you will join them there."

King Idun's voice was clear again, but he still didn't look at Sumer. Sumer stepped forward, keeping his eyes on his father's face.

"Will you join us, Father?" His face held hope.

"No elder shall pass the Golden Gates" said King Idun. "There are three rules of the wall, and this is one of them."

"Why, Father?"

King Idun blinked and looked at Sumer as if he just now realized who he spoke to.

"When the Qazams came from the north of the low river, High King Alm greeted us. We were few in numbers. He gave us homes and provided us with a place where we could live in generosity and peace.

He looked around the room, seeing in the eyes of these young soldiers the faces of their forefathers. They deserved to hear this story.

"As we adjusted to these lands, we learned the rules of the Golden Gates," he said. "Each tribe in the north made a rule that other tribes will live by. The Norms set the first rule, which is that none shall battle or over turn the Golden Gates. The High King set the second rule, which is that no soul who visits south of the Golden Gates and returns shall ever leave again. The king of the Qazams made the third rule."

The honor hall grew completely silent as King Idun looked around the room once more.

"The Qazam King shall not pass the Golden Gates," said King Idun.

The young Qazams in the honor hall looked at each other. Confusion filled their faces, but they didn't say anything. King Idun glanced at Sumer, who looked as bewildered as his fellow soldiers.

Someday, I'll tell you why, King Idun thought. I made this rule to protect my children, but fate was cruel to me. Because I made this rule, I am a prisoner here, and I send you into the danger I would like to have protected you from.

He shook his head, wishing he had the courage to say what was in his heart. Instead, he turned back to the soldiers.

"Go and say farewell to your families,
he said. "You shall leave when the moon hangs low."

As the Qazams left, buzzing with anticipation and curiosity about the final rule, Sumer looked for Aysha. He found her standing next to an open window.

"Are you scared? Because I know I would be," Aysha said. "I expected your father to say he would come with you."

"I'm not worried," Sumer said. "I just never dreamt of this day. I am honored to have a chance to follow in Lovnor's footsteps, but I'm also anxious about being away from home and away from my father. I'm anxious about being away from you, too."

"Come on now, how bad can it be down in the Middle-lands?" Aysha smiled wide, as if her encouragement could take away all Sumer's fear, but he still looked serious.

"My brother died down there," he said. "So did a lot of other Qazams. There was a lot of bloodshed during the Golden Age." His face paled. "I will be alright. I just need some time to think about this." He touched her arm briefly and turned, walking quickly away. Aysha's smile slipped off her face.

"I am sorry, Sumer," she called after him. "I didn't mean to offend you in any way."

Grief and despair echoed in the sound of Sumer's boots as he walked away.

"Don't worry, Sumer," she whispered under her breath. "Your father can't come with you, but I will find away. As a woman, I am not allowed to join the fighters, so I will cut my hair and go as a man."

She ran home, racing past the courtyard and the statute of King Idun. A few tree branches further, she burst into the home where her parents sat waiting for her, eager to hear the news from the honor hall.

"Aysha," said her mother, "What did the king say?"

Aysha's father stood, moving closer to hear her better, but Aysha barely noticed. She scrambled around the house, throwing a knife, a coat, and some food into a bag. She swung her sword onto the sheath she wore on her back before her mother was able to stop her.

"Honey, what are you doing?" Aysha's mother asked.

"The King said Sumer is marching the fighters of Qazam to city of Mik-Mag," said Aysha. She began hunting for more supplies while her father and mother whispered to each other.

"Another war?" Shock filled their faces, and finally Aysha's mother seemed to understand.

"If they are leaving, then what you are doing—my sweetheart, why are you collecting these items? Oh, no, you do not think you are going south, do you?"

Anger replaced her bewilderment. Aysha's father reached out and grabbed Aysha by the shoulders.

"Aysha, what you think you are doing? The land south of the Golden Gates is not a place for a Qazam woman. Do you hear me?"

"I won't let my love of Sumer die," Aysha said.

Her parents looked at each other, and then at Aysha.

As the moon hung low over the Qazam woods, the bright blue lights of Qazam homes illuminated the trees. Below them, the army of the Qazams stood firmly in two lines. They wore white and golden attire and carried bows.

King Idun and Queen Meltôriel walked side by side out of the great wooden castle. As King Idun watched, Meltôriel stepped gently down the stairs to the front of the army, where she began to give each young Qazam soldier a glowing blue flower.

"This ember of light shall help you find your way back home," she told each of them.

When she reached Sumer, who stood near the back of the army, Meltôriel tried to hold back tears.

"You look so much like Lovnor in this attire," she said.

"I still don't know how to lead the Qazams like he did," Sumer said.

"He was young and nervous, as you are," she said. "Do not be afraid. We shall always be by your side."

"Of course, my mother," said Sumer. He kissed her on the cheek and moved to the head of the army. The Qazam kin on both sides of the road watched as Sumer gave the forward shout.

"History is repeating itself," one woman wailed. "We do not know if we will ever see our children again."

Sumer scanned the crowd as the army passed by.

"Did you see Aysha?" he asked his friend, Valier. "I didn't get to say goodbye to her."

"No," Valier said. "I thought she would be here. It seems like everyone else is."

"That's strange. I haven't seen her since the meeting at the honor hall. I hope she's okay."

The words were too weak for the emotions Sumer felt. To leave without seeing Aysha once more was breaking his heart. His chest hurt. He scanned the crowd once more, but he couldn't see her face.

The families of the Qazam soldiers, the elders, Queen Meltôriel and King Idun watched while their sons marched through the trees, disappearing from view.

"I never thought this day would come," King Idun said. He turned to his queen and caught her hand. "You know who we have to go talk to."

They turned toward the Tower of Light and stepped toward it, followed by a handful of guards.

CHAPTER SEVEN –
The High King's Forest

Creatures from the Golden Age lived in the High King's forest. In the beginning of the silver age, some said that a great Madaul still resided there, but no one really knew.

There was a small cabin on the far side of the forest, where Adu, the brother of High King Alm, lived a quiet, focused life.

Unlike the High King, Adu had never married. He hadn't gone to the Middle-lands or to the far east, to the Land of the Unknown. Still, he had the same glow that his brother radiated, as if a torch lit his face from the inside. Even his long, gray beard emanated light.

Adu was tasked to train the High King's sons. The princes Umar, Adn, and Kaf had all spent time with him. After they left, he was given the responsibility to train Ismail, the High King's youngest son.

The past ten years had gone quickly. The odd cabin, with its grass-covered roof and small, uneven windows, had seemed more comforting than practical.

Adu turned the golden knob on the red door leading to the cabin's tiny courtyard. There was an old bird nest there and a chair where he sat when he gazed into the night sky.

When the sun went down and the moon hung low, the entire skyscape seemed to fill with awe. From his chair, one side of the sky appeared completely dark, while the other side was fully bright from the light of the tower.

Just now, the light from the tower mingled with daylight above the forest canopy, and a small herd of deer stepped gingerly through the bushes behind the cabin. Adu smiled as a young boy crashed through the forest, startling the deer into flight.

"Ismail. Here comes my Habibi," said Adu.

A songbird settled in a tree branch, creating a darker silhouette against the bright blue of the sky. It chirped at Adu, seeking his attention, but Adu's royal white eyes were focused on Ismail.

The short, skinny boy ran quickly, emerging from the woods with a small bag on his back and a short sword in his hand.

"Ismail. Don't run with a sword in your hand," Adu called. "I've told you before."

Ismail blinked his white eyes and smiled, brushing his long black hair away from his shoulders.

"My Baladay, how are you today?" Ismail's voice was pleasant, but he was breathless from running.

"Why did you go to the forest without me?" Adu tried to look stern, but it took a lot of effort. "Creatures live there that we've never talked about. They're dangerous. If you get in trouble with them and I don't know where you are, how can I help you?"

"I think I'm old enough to travel in the high woods alone," Ismail said. "I've been waiting for years."

Adu laughed. "Of all the kin that have come here to train, you are my favorite," he said. "Now come inside, and let's eat. I have some interesting news from the Tower of Light."

He led Ismail back into the cabin, where a handmade lamp swung from the middle of the ceiling. Its bright light mixed with the sunlight pouring in from the large front windows.

Ismail sat on a small, wooden seat near a heavy table.

"I hope my brothers are coming to visit me," he said. "I have not seen any of them in ten years. Much has happened since they left. I'd like to show you how much I learned from my Baladay."

Adu smiled, and Ismail chattered on.

"Baladay, what is the news from the Tower of Light? Are they sending new kin to train with me? Or is it as I hope? Are my brothers coming to visit?"

Adu stepped around the fireplace, where brown rice and soup bubbled in pots hanging over the fire. He picked up the open letter.

"I wanted to tell you this morning, but you ran off so early I didn't get the chance to."

Ismail looked down. "I'm sorry, my Baladay."

Adu cleared his throat and began reading.

"My dear brother, I am sending my best wishes for your health and well-being.

"I hope Ismail has not been bother nor a thorn in your side. He has much to learn from you, but the time has come to call him home. Please come with him to continue his training here. I plan to groom him to be the next king's guard, to protect our kingdom from any harm that might come upon us.

"May we see each other again soon, and may peace fill our lands.

"Your dear brother, Alm."

Adu laughed as he folded up the letter, and his face grew red. "It seems your father is missing us," he said.

"I never heard him say he missed me," Ismail said. "It's been so long since I saw my family and my fellow kin. Do you think they will remember me?"

Ismail thumped the table beside him absent-mindedly. Unhappiness filled his voice. "Does he really think I will be able to be a good king's guard? Baladay, I don't want to be a king's guard."

Adu lifted the cauldrons of soup and rice carefully from the iron bar where they hung and placed the on the table.

"What did I say about thinking too much?" Adu said. "Let's eat."

Ismail sullenly thumped a ladle-full of soup into a bowl.

"Listen," Adu said. "Your father did not say how long we can take to get there. We'll take our time rather than rushing. Would you like that?" Adu put an enormous spoonful of rice into his mouth, and a few grains dropped onto his beard.

Ismail spooned some rice into his bowl.

"We're having brown rice again," he said. "I see it every day."

"What's wrong with brown rice?" Adu laughed. "It's a good source for fiber and carbs, and a growing boy like you needs those things."

Ismail looked up. "You're right, Adu. I'm sorry. I'm just unhappy because the Tower of Light isn't really my home. I hardly even remember being there. The king's guards are all elder kin who fought in the Golden Age. What are they going to think of me coming back and taking a spot there?"

He took small bites of rice and soup while Adu filled their cups with buttermilk made from sheep milk.

"I understand, but you're the son of the king," Adu said. "They will be honored to have a royal person like yourself join their ranks. What is it about being a king's guard that bothers you so much? You would be your father's right hand. The people love him, and they will love you, too."

"I'm not sure I'm ready for this."

"Don't forget, I trained the current king's guards, just as I have trained you," Adu said. "Just because they have more experience than you, doesn't mean you won't belong. And do not forget, I'll be there with you."

A smile pulled on the corners of Ismail's mouth.

"Adu, you know just what to say, and that's why I love you so much," Ismail said. "I've learned so much being here with you, and I'll never forget it, but you should know that something beyond this forest is calling me. If I become a king's guard, I won't be able to find out what it is."

"You are nothing like your brothers or your father," Adu said. "You're everything like your mother, though. She never wanted to be trapped in a castle. Sometimes, looking at you, it's like she's here all over again."

"I miss my mother," Ismail admitted between bites. "I was only two when she passed away. She used to sing to me every night, but I hardly remember her voice now."

"Don't be sad, Ismail," Adu said, but even he swallowed hard and blinked. "Your mother is surely in heaven, smiling down upon us. If you only knew what this world really holds, and what the soul of a vessel really means..."

Adu's voice trailed off. Ismail waited, but when Adu didn't speak again, he set his bowl on the table and leaned forward.

"What do you mean, Baladay?" he asked.

Adu blinked again, shaking himself out of some private reverie. "Living does not stop, just because someone is dead. A soul is ever-living, even if the flesh of the body is gone. A soul is not in need of a body, but a body is in need of a soul. Your mother lost her body, but not her soul, and maybe she found a new—"

A jarring set of pounding knocks on the red door caused the glass in the front windows to rattle. Adu and Ismail looked up from their bowls with open mouths.

"Open up!" A loud voice from outside demanded.

"Who is that?" Ismail jumped out of his chair, grabbing his sword and bag.

"Do not move. Let me look." Adu slipped quietly to the large window and peered outside. His face grew pale.

Someone moved outside. Adu jumped back as the window shattered. Someone had thrown a torch. It smashed through the glass, landing on the floor at Adu's feet.

"Use the back door," Adu said. "You need to run, now!"

"Get outside now, or you will burn alive," said the loud voice from outside.

"Ismail, GO!" said Adu, shoving Ismail's pleading hands away. "I'm going to stay here and buy you some time."

"I'm not leaving here without you, Baladay!" said Ismail

"You leave now!" Adu hissed. "This is my job, and we both know it." He picked Ismail up, rushed him to the back door, and threw him out the window at the back of the cabin.

"No, Baladay, we can leave together! Please stop and let me help!" Ismail jumped to his feet, fighting to pull Adu through the window, but he was no match for Adu's strength.

"Run east, into the forest," Adu whispered. He slammed the window shut and locked it, and Ismail watched as his uncle ran back toward the front of the cabin.

The floor was already burning. Adu began shouting obscenities at the unseen foe in front of the cabin, keeping him focused on the inside of the house.

"Baladay!" Ismail cried. "Please come with me! Baladay!"

He tried to jump back up to the window, but he was too short, and the back door of the cabin was locked. He kicked against the door.

"Baladay! Baladay, no! Please come with me!"

The fire inside the cabin became a raging inferno. Smoke swirled from under the back door and through every crack between the cabin logs. Everything felt hot.

"Baladay, come out!" Ismail yelled again. "I need you!"

The grass on the roof withered and smoked. The beams holding it up were aflame. Ismail sobbed, almost missing the sounds of enemy voices from around the corner of the house.

"Those scum should be dead or dying inside," the loud voice said. "Once the fire has died down, go inside and find me those royal gems."

Ismail clutched his chest. He walked backward a few steps, hiding behind a tree while he caught his breath.

"What now? I cannot leave Adu, but maybe he is already dead. Those bastards must pay, but I'm alone. What would Baladay do?"

Tears streaked down his cheeks as he looked eastward, deep into a section of the woods where Adu had never taken him. He started to run. The smoke and sounds of flaming wooden beams faded behind him.

Within half an hour, he was lost. This section of the forest was old and abandoned. Strong roots wove through decayed buildings and broken statues of some forgotten royal family.

At least these were signs of civilization. Through his tears, Ismail reasoned that following the statues might take him to the nearest village. He slowed to a walk, sniffling and wiping his cheeks with the back of his hand.

In the far distance, a tower rose above the trees. A chimney poured black smoke into the air. Ismail saw this from the top of a ridge, and he rushed toward it, hoping still to find help for Adu.

It felt like an eternity before he finally burst into the clearing where the tower stood. A sign in the middle of the tower's entry read "Haeinsa."

"Haeinsa?" Ismail's voice rasped in his throat. He stared at the sign for a moment and then rushed into the tower, stumbling up a mountain of steps that spiraled upward.

"Hello? Help! I need help!" Ismail shouted as he ran up the steps. Why did no one answer?

As the stairs rose, the light from the windows below faded, and the tower grew dark. He felt his way to the top. There was a room there, but no windows and no candle to light his way.

Ismail felt his way around the room. It seemed full of tables piled with scrolls and letters. As his eyes grew used to the dim light, he saw that the room seemed to be abandoned. Letters were scattered across the floor, as if the previous occupants had left in a hurry.

A bell echoed in the distance. Ismail followed its sound through a narrow door that led into another small room. This one was filled with the dead bodies of thin, bald-headed monks in full orange cloaks. They lay shoulder to shoulder on the floor.

As Ismail made his way around the room, he was startled to see one small, pale face gazing right at him. Ismail froze, then walked forward again. The eyes from the unknown face followed him as he drew close.

"Are you dead or alive?" Ismail whispered. "If you're alive, I need help."

The face shifted as the monk, who was not even as old as Ismail, slowly rose to a sitting position. "I'm alive. Are you the next oath keeper, or merely a pawn of fate?"

Ismail took a step back, unsure what to say. The boy monk spoke again.

"I think you are the oath keeper. I'm Sarvajna. I have been waiting for you for a long time."

"What is an oath keeper?" Ismail whispered, as the monk stood.

"I've been waiting for you for a long time," Sarvajna said. "We were the monks of the north. We helped hold back the darkness, but our time has ended, and the darkness is rising now."

Sarvajna held out a hand, but he didn't touch Ismail. His voice sounded thin and worried. He looked deep into Ismail's eyes.

"Oath-keeper, you are the last hope," the monk said. "You must ride south and fight back the Curse of Darkness, so that the light does not fade."

"I don't understand," Ismail said. "I just want to help my uncle."

"The monks of the north saw this land of Amer cycle through many times of dark and light, but now times are turning, and hope is fading," Sarvajna said. "If the Tower of Light fades, the land of Amer will always be covered with pitch darkness."

Sarvajna's eyes were red from crying or lack of sleep, and his lips were white as though he hadn't had anything to drink in many moon-passes. He was a pitiful sight, but Ismail had other things on his mind.

"This too much to take in," Ismail said. "I just lost my uncle, and I need help. Please, do you know how I can get to the king's road from here? Maybe there I can get some help."

"I understand your pain," Sarvajna said. "I understand, but I think if your uncle was here, he would say...a soul is just a vessel, and not in need of a body."

Ismail froze again, shocked. "How could you know what my uncle told me just this morning?" His voice grew louder, strengthened with a sudden anger. "I'm only a child. Why are you tasking me with stopping the darkness?"

He stared at Sarvajna, who stared back, and Ismail found compassion for the scared and lonely young monk.

"Let me help you out of here," Ismail said. "Maybe then we can talk about this,"

"Fear not, oath-keeper, this is your time," Sarvajna said. He trembled. "Many will aid you in this quest. I have seen it. You must travel to a cave close to the Qazam lands. There you will meet the candle-maidens. They can assist you, if it suits you."

"You see this?" Ismail shook his head. "How can you be so sure? Neither my father nor my uncle ever told me of monks in the High King's Forest."

Sarvajna's blank stare unnerved Ismail, but the young monk's voice softened a bit.

"The High King was tasked with the same quest as you are, but he failed," Sarvajna said. "Now the curse grows, turning this world into chaos. Beasts and Jinn are coming in large numbers. More and more Norms are talking deceitfully. They bring demons up from the depths. These demons take dark forms and whisper in the ears of anyone who might listen, always working to kill the innocent Norms and Jinns."

"We were always taught that a boy would come," Sarvajna continued. "We did not know whether you would come from the west, the south, the east or the north, but here we are in these forgotten lands. You are fleeing from the raider Norms who killed your Baladay. I simply stayed here, stuck in this cycle of death with no food or water. It is fate that our paths are now crossing, whether you believe it or not."

Sarvajna took a deep breath and shifted his weight. He reached out again, and this time, his cold, think hand rested on Ismail's shoulder.

"Remember, Oath-keeper, a day will come when you must choose between your family and kin or saving the light, but the choice will always be yours."

Sarvajna blinked his eyes. He swayed on his feet, and his knees buckled. Ismail caught him and helped him sit again on the floor.

"The time of the monks is ending," the boy monk said. "I am fading now. I could only wait long enough for the oath-keeper to arrive. Ple-pleas-please save us, or this curse will swallow us whole, as it has so many others."

Sarvajna's breath came in shallow bursts. He closed his eyes, and Ismail helped him lay back against the floor. The young monk, the last monk of Haeinsa, stopped breathing. His hand grew limp and slipped off Ismail's shoulder, landing softly on the soft orange cloak.

Ismail stood. "How did you know about my Baladay?" he whispered, knowing Sarvajna could not answer. "How can I ever fight back this darkness?"

Ismail made his way back down the stairs, out of the tower of Haeinsa and into the woods, but he barely saw his surroundings. His mind was full of Sarvajna's words.

"How am I supposed to do this? And why is it supposed to be me, instead of Umar or Kaf or Adn?"

He followed the trail of broken statues, growing angrier with each step. As he stumbled along, he saw a large owl staring at him from the top of a nearby tree. His temper broke.

"Get away!" he shouted, and he plucked a stone from the forest floor and threw it at the owl's head.

His baladay's training was true. The rock hit the owl in the head. The owl screeched and flapped its wings.

"That hurt!" said the owl "What's the matter with you, boy?"

Ismail, startled by the owl's voice, stumbled backward and tripped over a tree root. "You can talk?"

"You can understand me?" the owl said, and he sounded as surprised as Ismail felt. "You must have met Sarvajna. Those monks had these kinds of powers, but Sarvajna was the last of his kind." The owl blinked. "What is your name, boy?"

"I am Ismail, son of Alm."

The owl opened its massive wings and glided to the lowest branch on the tree.

"What is the son of the High King doing so far from home?"

"I'm looking for the king's road," Ismail said. "Can you help me?"

"Come. I'll take you where you need to go, boy."

"I just want to go home," Ismail said.

"Oath-Keeper, you won't have a home if you let this curse swallow us whole,' the owl said.

Ismail looked down at his feet as he pushed himself up from the ground, thinking.

"This quest was father's quest, but he failed," Ismail finally said. "I will do what I can. My baladay would have wanted it."

The owl flapped its mighty wings again.

"Come," the owl said. "We shall go to the home of the Qazams."

The owl took to the air, gliding between the trees. Ismail ran through the thick woods behind him, trying his best to keep up.

CHAPTER EIGHT –
The Uneasy Travels

As the Golden Cavalry reached the city of Mik-Mag, Prince Kaf's soldiers grew silent and somber. Mik-Mag was the closest Middle-land village to the Golden Gates, but even here the grass was dead and covered with a fine black dust. Nothing grew in the fields, and there was no livestock to be seen.

"What happened here?" Prince Kaf said softly, gazing around at the burnt town.

"Everything here is gone," said Zuda, one of the young Northern Kin. "Only those buildings in the distance look occupied."

The young prince Kaf dismounted. An uneasy feeling seemed to permeate from the scorched ground right through the soles of his boots. There was no light, not even when he looked north, toward the Golden Gates.

Reality began to sink in.

The clouds darkened above the cavalry, and from the distance, Kaf heard the terrible sound of screams and cries from the buildings beyond the burnt village.

"I see people in the distance," Zuda said, drawing his golden sword. "Get ready."

Kaf jumped back onto his horse, and his men moved into a V formation with Prince Kaf at its point. He seemed unfazed, but his dark hair hung low and loose around his face. In the darkness, it was difficult to tell what anyone felt.

Shapes moved in the distance and became the silhouettes of people swarming forward, crying out.

"Hold! Hold!" Zuda shouted.

As the silhouettes moved nearer, faint patches of colors began to show up in the dim light. The golden cavalry saw skinny people with bare feet, dirty hair and ripped brown clothes.

These were no soldiers. These were souls who were barely surviving.

"Wait! Those are mothers, with babies!" one young soldier said to Prince Kaf.

Kaf held his sword in the air. "Stand down!" he shouted, and his men sheathed their swords, slowly breaking formation. As the people reached the Golden Army, they began begging for food, for help. They touched the soldier's golden attire, picking at it, trying to grab a few golden items for themselves.

"What's happening?" one soldier asked, looking at Zuda, but Zuda was also getting mauled by starving families who wanted mercy and attention.

Zuda looked for Kaf, but in the darkness and the thickness of the throng, it was difficult to make out where he was.

"Where are you from?" one skeletal man asked.

"We're from the north," Zuda said, gently nudging his horse forward through the sea of people. "Move. Move." He pushed forward, dodging a group of children who were trying to snatch any item they could tear off him.

"Stop!" Zuda and a few of his men finally broke through the crowd. Prince Kaf was still a little way off, and he appeared to be speaking with a man who looked as if he should have been young. This harsh life had aged him prematurely.

As the soldiers move closer, the strange man reached out his hand to Prince Kaf. "We'll see you later," he said.

For Prince Kaf, the moment was terrifying and surreal. As the man's palm touched his, Kaf's sight grew dark with a vision. All around him, the land and sky were black, and it was too dark to make out shapes or color. In the distance, two eyes glowing with fire stared at him, and a whisper echoed in his mind.

"One day all the light will fade, and the darkness will become a curse in every land."

The man released Kaf's hand abruptly and moved back, vanishing in the crowd of locals.

Kaf opened his white eyes, which flickered fearfully into the throng.

"La-mutra. Find him," said Kaf.

Coven

CHAPTER NINE –
Coven

The journey from the Tower of Haeinsa was arduous, and both Ismail and the owl were weary when they finally reached the fork where the king's road split in three directions. By this time, the sun had set.

"I know about this road," Ismail said. "Father always spoke about the three roads that the Norms built in the Golden Age."

The owl fluttered to the top of a tree near the fork in the road. "Yes, these roads have been here since ages past," he said. "But we shouldn't rest here long. Follow me."

The owl dropped from the tree and glided toward the Qazam forest. Ismail trotted behind, watching as the stars and moon emerged. They were bright that night, even with the light from the Tower of Light in the distance. As they made their way to the edge of the Qazam forest, even the trees lit up with a glowing blue aura.

Ismail struggled to keep up. Even with the light around him, it was difficult to keep the owl in his vision, and the forest was thick. Instead of gliding over the forest canopy, he had to wind between bushes, tree roots and fallen branches.

"Wait!" He finally called, as he pushed himself over a fallen tree.

The owl circled around and landed on the log.

"Aren't you able to climb over the branches?" asked the owl.

Ismail was tired, hungry and grieving, and his temper got the better of him. He snapped at the owl.

"Yes, but where are you going? I can't even see you half the time." His inner light dimmed dangerously. Even the owl knew to respect this, and he dared not tempt the boy any further.

"Climb onto my back," the owl said. "I'll fly you there, but if you speak of this to any one, I'll eat you."

Ismail glared, but he nodded and climbed onto the owl's back. The owl was bigger than himself, so he felt balanced and safe, but the feathers were rough and thick like leather.

The owl flapped his wings and rose into the sky, carrying Ismail over the Qazam forest. In the air, the light from the trees, the moon and the stars made the world seem to sparkle.

"Oh," Ismail said, catching his breath. "I've never seen moonlight like this. Do you see this beauty every night?"

"Yes," said the owl. "Remember this. This beauty is what we're fighting to protect. If you fail in your quest, the curse of darkness will cover and destroy everything beautiful in the land."

Tree-covered hills and then mountains rose in front of them. The owl flew toward a rocky cave high above the Qazam trees. Near the entrance of the cavern, he wheeled around and landed on the low-hanging branch of a half-fallen tree.

The cave was slightly covered with a few branches, but Ismail could still see it clearly. He scooted down from the owl's back and dropped onto the ground as the owl spoke.

"There you must go, but I cannot enter," the owl said.

"Why not? You flew me here, so why not come with me a little further?" Ismail looked up at the owl, and then faced the cave. "What's inside? Will anyone hurt me?" He took a step toward the entry.

"They might bite," the owl joked, but Ismail didn't think it was funny. He glared again at the owl, but he still stepped into the darkness of the cave.

There was no door. A table stood in the entry, and a candle on the table provided the only light in this dim room.

"Here comes the oath-keeper," said a small, old voice, and Ismail heard the soft cackling of two other old voices.

"You come, but you don't even know why," the first voice said. "That's how everyone comes to us, young boy. Come inside with us, and let me tell you a tale from days long forgotten."

An old woman stepped forward into the candle light. Her long blonde hair was adorned with red roses.

"My name is Marta. We are the candle-maidens. Don't be afraid."

She held out a hand to him and smiled. He walked toward her, but he didn't take her hand. Wind blew through the cavern opening. Somewhere in the distance a bell rang.

Beyond Marta, there were four chairs. Two of them were occupied with other old women. One of them knitted a coat with fine golden fur while the other drank a glass of wine. Marta sank into one of the two remaining chairs and invited Ismail to sit, as well.

"It is your fate to be here with us," Marta said. "We have been waiting for you."

"Yes, a long time," one of the other old ladies said. "We waited for many moon-passes, but finally you are here, oath-keeper. You are younger than we thought you would be, but there is no time for that now."

"Why?" Ismail asked. "Why am I here?"

The candle flickered more brightly, casting light and shadows on the red robes the candle-maidens wore.

"Why are any of us here?" One candle-maiden said, and Marta leaned forward in her seat.

"Young kin of the High King, all your choices in your life lead you here for a reason. A great danger brews in the south."

"Yes, but why am I here?" Ismail asked again. "Why is it me?"

The wind picked up again, and the sound of bells grew louder. Outside, the owl hooted.

"Oh, you brought Laenatan," a candle-maiden said, and they all laughed. "Poor soul. He's still flying around these lands, but it's good that he's here."

"Do you know him?" Ismail asked.

"Oh, yes," Marta said. "Yes, we do. He was once a human like you, but he denied this same quest in the first age, so we cursed him. We turned him into an owl. Since then, he has always wandered over these lands, never sleeping, and always thinking about the choice he made."

"He was a boy once?" Ismail glanced toward the opening of the cave, but he couldn't see the owl.

"Yes," Marta said proudly. "We turned him into an ever-living owl."

Ismail felt angry again. "Why? Why would you do that to him?"

"Do not get your temper up, young son of the High King," Marta said. "Laenatan's fate differs from yours. He was tasked to aid the first oath-keeper, who was your father, but Laenatan abandoned his task and fled into the eastern part of the High King's forest. When he showed his face to us again, we turned him into an owl. Now he roams these lands, and always will, until his oath is fulfilled."

The wine-drinking candle-maiden spoke up.

"You can help him, Oath-keeper," she said. "You can free his soul if you take this quest, and you must take this quest, lest this curse swallow us whole."

"As it has so many others," Marta said.

Ismail let silence wrap around him for several long breaths. When he spoke again, he sounded confused.

"My father never told us that he was tasked as an oath-keeper," he said. "Why would he hide this from us, and what happens now? How can I ever live up to my father, and his legacy?"

"We know," Marta said. "This might be hard to hear, but your father failed. Now his heir will take his place and finish what he could not."

"But how can I ever take this quest?" Ismail asked. "I do not know what to do. I don't know these lands. I don't even know how to pass the Golden Gates. Why can't we just pick someone else, like one of my brothers?"

Marta smiled. "Don't worry. Many will aid you in your quest, but first, you must rest. You must be tired." She beckoned for him to help her out of her chair.

"Come with me," she said, as he reached out and pulled her to her feet. She wobbled as though she had been sitting in one spot for ages. "Dear me. Oh, dear. Please, help me to my room," she said.

She nodded as Ismail picked up the candle. They left the other candle-maidens in darkness as they walked to Marta's room. Candlelight fell against the walls of the cave as Marta told Ismail the history of the candle-maidens.

"We've been living here since the Norms came during the first Golden Age," she said. "They came in mass numbers, running from battles that took place in Mik-Mag. I remember poor women holding their babies as they cried and fathers holding their youngest sons, begging the northern lands to let them in. In the distance, the watchers on the gate saw dark clouds in the south and lighting that glowed red and green. We have never seen lighting like that in the North."

"I never knew where the Norms came from," he said. "Until this morning, all I really knew about them was that they brought bags of brown rice to my Baladay and I every month. What must green and red lightning be like, if it's enough to drive them from their homes?"

"You cannot imagine it, can you?" Marta asked.

Ismail shook his head. "I have never seen rain nor dark clouds," he said. "What could cause such a storm?"

"Our Qazam kin were less likely to help the Norms," Marta said. "We didn't want them invading our land and cutting down our trees, but the High King said the refugees came to flee the killing that was occurring in the Middle-lands."

"Why was there any killing, anyway?" Ismail said.

"The Jinn were looking for a boy that they believed lived in the city of Mik-Mag," Marta said. "That statement was what started our watch for the oath-keeper. We thought your father was that boy. He was chosen to be our champion, but oh, we were mistaken. He was already old by that age, nearly 120 years old, and he had his own desires and hopes and dreams. He was ready to find love, and after he started the march to the south, he was lost to us."

They reached Marta's room, which was a simple dark room containing no items that any living normal person could use. Ismail helped Marta to her bed, and then he lay on the floor on the other side of the narrow room.

"La-Uma, La-Uma, La-Uma," Marta prayed. They both fell asleep with only the candle lighting the room.

CHAPTER TEN –
The Turn of the Tides

Horns blew and echoed across the plains as the rest of Prince Umar's army began marching south again, toward the burnt land of Mik-Mag. The men were fearless still, although less playful as the darkness grew thicker.

When the cavalry reached the peak of the hill overlooking Mik-Mag, Prince Umar and Prince Adn looked down across the valley. The land was burnt and singed everywhere.

"Kaf had better not be to blame for this," Prince Umar said. "Adn, do you see this?"

"I see it, but I don't understand it," Adn replied.

As the army marched past the princes, they caught the attention of Kaf and his men, who rode up to greet them joyously. The locals of Mik-Mag followed them, clinging like the fine black dust that coated everything.

"I'm happy to be reunited with my brothers," Kaf told Zuda as they rode. "I was glad to ride ahead at first, but I didn't expect to find anything as bleak and desperate as this burnt land."

"Umar looks pissed," Zuda said. "I'm not sure I want to stay and get yelled at." He slid off his horse and began walking among the locals, leading his horse along slowly.

"Why are they upset?" Kaf asked.

"I do not know, but you know how Prince Umar can be," Zuda said. He pulled away from Kaf, leading his horse to the left and trying to lose himself in the crowd.

Kaf looked ahead at the Golden Army, which was finally reaching the burned-out city. "My Prince," said one soldier as he rode past. "My Habibi," said another.

Kaf nodded, but his white eyes focused on his brothers as they drew close enough for him to see their faces, the green gems that Umar wore and his long red cape falling behind his horse as he rode.

"We told you to ride in front and scout the scene out, not burn it!" Umar yelled as he closed in.

"It was already like this when we got here," Kaf said.

Adn slowed, willing to reckon with Kaf, but Umar charged ahead.

"I don't care. Why is your army dismounted?"

Kaf didn't like the shouting, but he understood. The light of the north had faded, and the darkness was getting to everyone. He knew Umar would take any excuse to be angry now. It was better than being afraid.

"Stop," said Adn. "Why do you both fight? Umar, I believe it was like this before they got here."

"Fine!" Umar said. "Then what happened here? What did you learn from the locals?"

"We have been talking to the villagers for the past few days," Kaf said. "They say the land has been like this since the Ajud, and also that they get raided often from this Presit," Kaf said.

"Ajud and a Presit?" Adn rubbed his chin.

"Yes. I don't know what those terms mean, either," Kaf said.

Umar sat straight on his horse, hardening his face and ignoring the tiny flecks of mud on his lavishly embroidered cape. Finally, he rode over to a group of locals who stood under a distressed-looking burned out shed.

"Who are the leaders here?" he asked. "Who is the oath-keeper, and who is the Shah?"

"A king?" A high-pitched laugh burst from one of the locals. The group dissipated as a well-dressed man with a brown coat and well-kept hair stepped forward. He wore an arrogant smile.

"No kings or princes come here and demand answers," the man said, looking directly into Prince Umar's eyes. "Many say you're all fake pretenders and liars!"

The crowd was already on the man's side, and they were easily swayed by his antagonism.

"Yeah!" a local shouted, and he lunged close to Prince Umar, holding out a sharp knife. The locals shouted louder.

"People, let's take it easy," the well-dressed man said, pointing at the Golden Army. "They are just kids. We don't need to turn this into a blood bath, do we?"

He looked directly at Prince Umar. "These young men rode here from the north to protect us," he said, and then his voice grew cold. "But we don't need your protection, Marid children," the well-dressed man said.

Everyone stilled, even the locals who had been shouting and who had shuffled closer. The villagers stared at Umar on his horse, while the Golden Army focused on the well-dressed man and the villagers.

Prince Umar's voice filled with strength.

"We are no rebels, so do not call us Marid," he said. "Enough with the pleasantries! What is your name?"

The well-dressed man, who was still smiling and joking with the locals in the crowd, brushed the dust off his shoulders.

"My name is Cassini, but my friends call me Nagas," he said. "I'm not much for outsiders claiming to help us. We know how this goes. You come here on your fine horses, wearing your fine jewelry and golden attire, but you are only an army of kids."

Cassini's voice grew hard and cold again. "You think you're the first one to do this," he said. "We always get taken advantage of by people like you, so now it's my turn to ask questions. Who are you, and why have you come here, your highness?"

While he spoke, the locals of Mik-Mag began pushing in again, shoving up against the Golden Army's soldiers and their horses. They shouted their annoyance.

Umar paused, watching the crowd for a moment. His own men were beginning to shift uneasily on their horses. He knew all he could do was stay calm and speak the truth, just as his uncle Adu had taught him.

"I'm Prince Umar, the eldest son of High King Alm," he said. "We were tasked to come here and aid the Middle-lands. We were told to stop at the city of Mik-Mag first, because my O-Father was sent a raven with a note that requested our help."

The shifting paused again, and everyone looked at Prince Umar. Some of the locals gasped. They finally connected the golden attire, the long black hair and the slight glow coming off the kin of the north.

The locals began smiling, and then, they cheered.

"Welcome! Welcome, young princes!" Cassini's face changed completely as joy and relief overtook him. "We didn't dare hope you would come."

The cheering crowd grew louder, and the locals close to the soldiers now hugged them or patted their legs instead of threatening them.

Only one person, huddling in the corner of the old shed, didn't seem excited. The strange man who had frightened Kaf with the vision stood, muttering to himself.

"Well, this just got interesting. Wait until the Oligarchs hear of this."

He ran to a hobbled horse, freed it and climbed onto its back. "Oh, I can't wait to let the saint know," he said. "He might even give me some old coins for this information."

The strange man inched away slowly, carefully, so that he didn't arouse suspicion. He didn't need to worry. Swarms of people cheered the young princes as he reached the gates and began galloping south down the road, away from the city.

The locals led the young princes into the nicest building they had. It was still a crumbling mess, but it appeared sturdier than the buildings around it.

"Come inside," the locals said. "Now that we know who you are, we're honored to host you."

The Golden Army marched behind the princes. As they drew near, the princes saw a sign above the doors.

Welcome to El Dorado, the sign read.

Kaf looked at Adn. "El Dorado?" he asked.

"Your guess is as good as mine," Adn said. "I've never heard of El Dorado."

They passed through the wooden doors, into a brightly lit hall filled with candles and hanging lanterns. In the center of the floor and around the room, the space made up an enormous bazaar.

It was a busy place. People argued as they exchanged goods for coins. Customers plead and bargained for reasonable prices. There was a strong scent of spices brewing, and there were booths selling weapons and armors.

There were also wild animals kept in cages, ready to be sold as pets. Heavily-furred lions, whose fur was dark and dirty, were shackled around their necks. Glass bins held long, dark snakes with green venom dripping from their fangs. There were even some unknown creatures from the Nabatean Mountains, but only a few merchants had birds to sell.

One of the bird vendors seemed to have birds of every kind. His booth was filled with cages of hawks, pigeons, and owls, and on his table was the egg of a roc. This attracted Umar's attention. He stopped to look at this ancient bird egg.

"You have eggs of roc birds?" he asked. "Those legendary birds died out hundreds of years ago from a plague. My uncle had one, but it's dead now, too."

The merchant looked at Umar. He seemed nervous, and his smile was strained.

"We do not ask those kinds of questions, my friend," said the vendor, "But if you want to know more, they're from a guy in West-land who can answer your questions." He smiled wide and turned to the crowd milling past. "Birds for sale! Birds for sale! Small birds, message birds!"

"That's unbelievable," Umar said to himself. "Uncle Adu always said those were the biggest birds he had ever seen."

The soldiers walked through the bazaar behind Umar. They seemed overwhelmed by the sights and sounds, the fascinating goods and the loud shouts of merchants trying to get their attention.

"Will you buy spices from the West-lands, or have a fine wine from the great city of Minar? Or maybe you would like fruit from Khali. They are the best fruits the land of Amer has to offer," one seller said, pulling at the hands of a passing soldier.

"No, we do not need anything," the soldier said.

The merchant's face fell. "Please, buy something. I have not sold anything in months. My children need to eat." The vendor held his hands together, begging for a sale. Most of the soldiers walked past him, but a few stopped to see what he carried.

"Welcome, my brothers. My name is Sohab. if you have any questions, my brother, just ask me." The merchant's voice filled with the joy of hope.

Zuda walked around the seller's booth, intrigued by the wide variety of merchandise dangling from the walls.

"Where did you purchase these things?" Zuda asked. "You have a stack of scrolls and old jugs and plates—and you have a golden sword?" Zuda's mouth fell open as he lifted an ancient sword from the table in front of him.

"We don't ask these kinds of questions, my friend," said Sohab. "El Dorado has been here for hundreds of years. Items come and go. Sometimes large armies pass by here, and you would be surprised at what they leave behind, but that golden sword never left this place."

Zuda fingered the golden sword. It was similar to his own, but burnt and dirty. The blade was still sharp, though.

"That sword has been here for years," Sohab said. "No one knows where it came from, but the elders say a great battle happened here during the Golden Age. My friend, I see you have a similar sword. Maybe you would like to have this one for a back-up."

Zuda nodded.

"For you, my friend, it will cost two hundred gold coins."

The background was noisy, and Zuda was growing hot. He didn't even bargain with Sohab. He just wanted to pay and leave.

"Fine," said Zuda. He pulled out a sack of golden coins and placed it on the table in front of Sohab.

Sohab smiled. "You made a great choice, my friend," he said. "You enjoy it, alright?"

Zuda pushed through the crowd, and Sohab began yelling again at other soldiers as they passed by.

In a less busy corner of the bazaar, Zuda took the sword out again and began to examine it. Something about it made him feel odd.

"How could it be a sword from the north, here in this marketplace?" he wondered.

He spotted Prince Adn a few booths away, and he went to show him what he purchased.

"My prince," Zuda said. "I bought a sword from that seller over there. It's the same as ours, but old and burnt. The merchant said it's been here for years, following a battle that too place here. I was hoping you might know its legacy."

"Let me look," Adn said. "It should have a signature on it."

Adn took the sword and looked for a signature. It was damaged from fire, but under the golden handle was a small engraving of HQ.

"HQ?" said And, looking at Zuda. "I don't know what that means.". They walked away from the market, still pondering what the answer could be.

The candle-maidens

CHAPTER ELEVEN –
Friend or Foe

The candle in Marta's cave room burned low, and Ismail woke to see the most beautiful girl he had ever seen watching over him. For a moment, all he could do was stare at her amazing green eyes, her long blonde hair and the most pointed ears he ever saw.

"You're a Qazam?" he said, sitting up and straightening his attire.

"Yes," she said. "Who are you?"

"I'm Ismail. Umm, why are you here? I mean, how long have you been here?"

Secretly, he wondered why a girl this magnificent would be in such a dark and creepy place. He also hoped he hadn't been snoring in his sleep.

"I live here," she said. "I've been living here for a few years now. I intend to learn how to be a candle-maiden, but so far, I just clean up and take care of the maidens," she said.

"Why?" asked Ismail. "I mean, I really don't know what they do, but it seems lonely."

Marta walked into the room with drinks and a new candle in her hands. "Oh, you're awake, and I see you met my grand-daughter, Nimra."

"She's your grand-daughter?" Ismail could hardly believe that someone so beautiful could have descended from Marta's old body.

"You're shocked," Marta said, laughing. "Well, I used to be a real cutie in my youth, and I wasn't lonely, so speak for yourself. You lived with your uncle in the woods, right? I bet that was lonely."

She handed Ismail and Nimra drinks and small bowls of white rice. As he ate, Ismail wondered how Marta knew about his uncle. Pangs of grief flooded up inside his heart, but he shoved them back down. No matter how much he hurt, he didn't want to make a fool of himself in front of Nimra.

"What is this orange drink?" he finally asked. It has an odd taste. It's both sweet and sour."

Nimra and Marta looked at each other and laughed.

"We make that," Nimra said. "I would not ask too many questions, or you won't want to drink it."

"Um. Okay," Ismail said. He stumbled over his words every time he looked at Nimra. "How many are you? I mean, how many candle-maidens are there?"

"There were many of us, throughout the years," Marta said. "The candle-maidens have always waited for the oath-keeper, but many perished, and some just gave up. There are only three of us now, and Nimra."

She paused, rubbing a hand across her cheek thoughtfully.

"Some say the western lands have their own candle-maidens, but who really knows?" she said.

She stood and held the candle in front of her, leading Ismail and Nimra back toward the other candle-maidens.

"Come, Ismail," Marta said as they walked. "I have something to give you, if it pleases you to take this quest."

"You still did not tell you why you want to be a candle-maiden," Ismail said to Nimra as they followed her grand-mother.

"It wasn't my choice" said Nimra. "My grandmother said this is my fate, and she brought me here from my home in the Qazam trees."

"You don't really seem happy by this," he said.

Before she could reply, they entered the entry room, where the other candle-maidens still sat. They immediately began picking on Ismail.

"Oh, here comes the oath-keeper and another cursed one," one of them said, and they both giggled.

"Stop it, ladies," Marta said, and they quieted at once. "Come, Ismail, sit down."

He sat down and looked beyond Marta to where the bright light of morning's first sunbeams poured through the cave entrance. Nimra stood beside the opening, peering out into the sunlight.

"We have a map for you," Marta said. "This map will show you how to pass the Golden Gates unseen. There are caves underneath the Golden Gates that will lead you to the western lands. Remember, you cannot get caught by any of the soldiers or watchers at the Golden Gates. Your father cannot find out about this quest."

"Why not?" asked Ismail. "I would like to see my father before I go."

"Time has hardened the High King's heart," she said, "But he will always want to protect you. If he finds out what you're doing, he'll never let you pass the Golden Gates, and the darkness will spread across these lands. Without you, it will swallow us whole, as it has so many others."

Marta's eyes suddenly looked tired and sad. After a wait of hundreds of years, the candle-maiden's purposes all came to this moment.

"Remember, oath-keeper, if you take this quest many will aid you, but they may not know why."

Ismail looked around the room, trying to think. Even the idea of eternal darkness was slowly breaking him down. He fought despair as well as grief.

"But I cannot do this alone," he said. "Even with a map, I'm afraid I won't know the way. Where do I need to go, and what exactly do I need to do?"

"Those are good questions," Marta said. She pulled out an ancient crown with three green gems on it. "Here, you'll need this."

Ismail examined the crown. It hadn't aged well, but the three green gems were still bright. They appeared to have a small glow about them.

"What is this?" he asked.

"This has been here for years, ever since we began waiting for the oath-keeper," Marta said. "This crown will help you. It's a sign of the oath-keeper. The green gems were a gift from the Dragon King of the western lands."

"The Dragon King?" Ismail lifted his face, searching Marta's eyes for more information.

"Yes, but the dragons never leave their mountains in the far western lands," she said. "You must go there first to get a sword that will aid you in the upcoming war."

"Why me?" Ismail asked again. "Why not someone stronger than me, or much older?"

"This is your fate, young prince, the son of light," Marta said. "It is your responsibility to fight back the darkness, but the choices you will make are the reasons why your fate is sealed. So, it is with your brothers."

"What about my brothers?" said Ismail, and an uneasy feeling flowed through his body.

"There's no time to go into that," Marta said. "However, I won't send you without help. Nimra will go with you."

Nimra turned away from the cavern entrance, and her voice held her surprise. "I will?" She smiled, as if she was as delighted as she was startled, and Ismail's heart lifted a little.

"I told you, Nimra, this is your fate," Marta said. "You will aid the oath-keeper and help him reach the dragon hills."

"Head to the cave far west of the Golden Gates," said the continuously-knitting candle-maiden. "You'll find a cave underneath that leads to the western lands. Take the owl with you."

"That sounds like a good idea," Marta said.
"He should be able to assist you in your journey to the Castle of Blayney. Once you make it under the gates, it should only be a few days traveling west before you find a scholar. He'll be able to aid you further on your quest."

All the candle-maidens nodded in agreement, and Marta sent Nimra to pack bags for the travelers. While she was gone, she turned to Ismail again.

"Remember, Oath-keeper, this darkness is not just a cloud that blocks the sun. This darkness brings a curse that turns all people into mindless shells. If you spend too much time in it, you'll lose yourself, as many others have."

She reached out and patted his arm. "If you see dark clouds and hear whispers of the cursed ones, run or fight the darkness," she said. "Only you can stop it from spreading into the northern-lands, but worrisome tales are coming from the West-lands, too. Stay near the main road to the West-lands, and do not trust anyone."

Nimra returned with empty satchels and baskets of food, water, pans and dried fruit. Ismail rose from his chair and began to help pack.

"Was this your plan all along?" Nimra asked her grandmother, when Ismail was distracted.

Marta looked sad. "Even though I predicted your fate, somehow I thought this day would never come," she said.

"I trained every day, but I don't know if I'm really ready," Nimra said. "I'm uneasy. This is such a big task."

"You will be ready when the time comes. I have foreseen it," said Marta. She smiled as she reached her arms around Nimra, hugging her tightly. "You take care, my beautiful princess."

"Okay," Ismail said behind them. "I'm ready. Are you all set?" He moved forward slowly, balancing the huge bag on his back. A few items bulged or poked out of the sides here and there, but he managed not to fall over.

"Yes, I'm ready," said Nimra. They walked out of the cave and into the bright light of morning. The candle-maidens sat in the darkness, listening to the breeze blow through the trees and the songbirds as they flitted around.

"You know, Ibies will be looking for him every single step they take," said one of the candle-maidens.

"I know," said Marta. She looked toward the cavern entrance, as if she almost hoped the young oath-keeper and Nimra would return.

Saint Lawrence

CHAPTER TWELVE –
Chains and Shackles

Below the dark gray clouds, the trees were dead or dying. The grass was brown. Crows fed on the dead.

The darkness in these lands spread evil, so that only despair filled the hearts of men here. The poor were crowded into jails as the dark-armored soldiers of Ibies marched around the damp Tower of Hasiphane. Here, the sun-rays never reached through the clouds, and unspeakable things happened to the helpless.

As the strange man who frightened Kaf reached the tower, he shifted in his saddle uneasily. Norms from the Middle-lands were being tortured. Their screams and pleas for an early death hung in the air. Their fates were sealed.

The entry was adorned with hanging heads and a sign reading 'Muslakh.' Slaughterhouse. Soldiers stopped the man here.

"I'm here to see St. Lawrence," the man said, edging carefully off his horse. He put his hands in the air, hoping that the soldiers wouldn't take him to the dungeons underneath the tower.

Ingie, the captain of the soldiers in this horrible place, glared at the man.

"Why? Why should we listen to you? You should leave here, if you know what's best for you."

Another scream of horror echoed in the courtyard, and the stench of death filled the air. The strange man gagged involuntarily. Many people who entered these black gates vanished, and no one asked why.

He glanced up at the tall rock walls reaching the clouds above him. Over the years, the darkness had spread from the south into the Middle-lands, and even far west, but this place was still a stronghold of evil.

The tower of Hasiphane was the first of the seven dungeons to be built beyond the home of Ibies, in the south. Only the Oligarchs knew what happened at the home of Ibies. They were tasked by him to spread his evil and destroy anyone who questioned his rule. That was why the Oligarch called St. Lawrence had built Hasiphane.

Now it stood as a beacon of darkness and horror. The strange man standing at its gates trembled.

"Leave this place," said Ingie, "Or else—"

"No need for that." A stately man with long white hair and spotless white robes descended the tower stairs. His voice was powerful, and even Ingie jumped.

"Saint Lawrence, do you know this man?" Ingie asked.

"Oh, yes. This is Hassen. He's one of Ibies' spies, one of the Khad from the Middle-lands." St. Lawrence's eyes glittered as he came closer. "The Khad group spies all across the land of Amer, but they never report to Oligarchs."

"Then why are you here?" Ingie turned back to the strange man.

Hassen ignored Ingie and spoke directly to St. Lawrence. "I have news that may interest you," he said. "May we speak privately?"

"Why are you not riding south still? You report to Ibies, not to me," St. Lawrence said.

"You know as well as I do," Hassen said. "If I ride south, I will never return."

St. Lawrence laughed. "Come inside, then," he said. "We'll talk in my chambers."

Hassen walked up the stairs behind St. Lawrence, ignoring Ingie's muttered insults and glares of distrust. The screams were louder inside the tower, and the scent of blood filled the air.

St. Lawrence appeared satisfied.

"Many don't come here by free will," he said, glancing at Hassen. "We take them in the night from their families. We take them when they are selling their goods. We take them while they are kicking and screaming."

He smiled at Hassen, who hid another gag behind the sleeve of his coat.

"I bet you know a lot of the Norms from the Middle-lands that fill these dungeons," St. Lawrence said. His voice grew stern. "Maybe you even know that boy, the one Ibies saw in a vision. He wants that boy, and anyone who might aid him."

Hassen swallowed. "That why I am here. I came here to the strong hold of Ibies in the Middle-lands to report that three of the princes from the North have marched to the city of Mik-Mag."

St. Lawrence paused, and a look of sinister happiness filled his face.

"If we get these princes, and take them to the south, Ibies would reward us with our delight, and I could leave this nightmare," he said.

They resumed walking, and as they neared the chamber of the saint, Hassen saw two red eyes on the door. He shuddered. Ibies watched everything in this area.

The chamber was filled with old scrolls and messages, books on the floor, and one chair, for the saint only. Hassen stood, watching as Saint Lawrence pulled out ink, a pen and a scroll.

Saint Lawrence always preached of peace to the Middle-land people, but he was a wolf in sheep's clothing. He spread the darkness as he sought more and more power. Hassen was still nervous about ending up as a prisoner of Hasiphane.

"So, tell me more about what you saw at Mik-Mag," the saint said. "Don't forget any details. I want to know everything."

"I did not see much, but I did speak to the young Prince Kaf. He told me they had never seen the Middle-lands before."

"Go on," Saint Lawrence said, scribbling away on the scroll. Hassen cleared his throat.

"They all wore golden attire, and they radiated light. I've never seen light emanating from anyone like that."

"Anything else?" said St. Lawrence, looking up from the scroll.

"Yes. The people are happy."

Anger glittered in St. Lawrence's eyes as he slammed his pen against the desk. "Happy?"

"Yes, they showed glad tidings to the young princes, once they knew who they were," Hassen said.

"Oh, they think they have hope?" said the saint. "No, they will have chains and shackles and they will pray for an easy death. I will hang them from their feet and cut them like sheep. Their blood will flow like streams in the streets."

He picked up his pen once more and wrote silently, ignoring the screams echoing up through the tower. Finally, he finished his note and looked at Hassen again.

"Anything else?" he asked.

"Yes," Hassen said. "They are there alone. There are no Qazams and no Norms from the north. These are only children playing at being men."

"Interesting. The High King is taking a big risk sending his heirs to the Middle-lands, but it does not matter now. We'll send a small force to the city, and you'll lead them." said the saint.

"Me?" Hassen looked sharply at the saint. "Why? I'm not a fighter, or a battle leader. That's why I spy," he said, trying to control the tone of pleading that crept into his voice.

"You speak as you have a choice. Remember, you came to me, so now you work for me, not just the Khad."

The saint smiled again. "I will send you with a small force, and I'll ride behind with my army to give those young pretenders a false sense of hope."

Hassen shook, both with anger and fear. The saint stood and faced him.

"I'll send a message to the other Oligarchs to share this information, but heed my warning, scum," Saint Lawrence said. "If you betray us, you'll have a much worse fate than what happens in any of our dungeons. Now go and see Ingie. Suit up and ride to the city of Mik-Mag."

Hassen could see no other option. "Of course, my saint," he said through gritted teeth. He left the Saint's chamber with a fervent hope to never return. Behind him, he heard the Oligarch laughing, calling out in a fearsome joy to anyone who might hear.

"This is my chance! I can take these scums of princes to Ibies, and he'll reward me. That will show those other Oligarchs. Those old bastards don't know when to die."

CHAPTER THIRTEEN – Who Leads Who?

"Do you know where you are going?" Nimra asked. "I swear, we have been in these woods for hours."

Ismail shifted his big bag of items and nodded forward. "Yes, I think it is this way."

They ran through the woods toward the High King's road. Around them, the trees reached as tall as their eyes could see, and houses made of wood were built into them.

"Try to avoid their attention," Nimra said, pointing out a group of Qazam soldiers.

They scrambled through thick bushes, swiping and the swarms of small bugs that seemed attracted to their heads. Before too long, they saw Norm writing on the ground.

"We're getting close to the main road," Ismail said. "It's a little more this way." He pushed through a thick stand of shrubs, where light glowed through leaves.

"I know this light," Ismail said. He started forward again, following the bright glow. They stepped out of the leaves and onto the plain.

"We made it," said Nimra. She smiled at the bright light from the Tower of Light in the northern distance. "I never thought we'd get out of those woods. I'm tired. Let's take a quick break."

She sat down a big rock near the High King's Road. Laenatan circled above, keeping an eye on Ismail and Nimra.

Ismail dropped onto the rock beside Nimra. "May I ask you something?" he asked.

"Of course, Oath-keeper," said Nimra.

Ismail winced. "Please do not call me that."

"What should I call you, then?" replied Nimra.

"Call me La-Pid," said Ismail, holding back a laugh.

"Wha...what does that mean?" Nimra's face twisted in confusion.

"It means small rat, Ismail said, and he laughed happily. Nimra only stared at him.

"It's not funny to you?" he asked, and he grew sober again.

"No," Nimra said. "I don't know why you like to be call La-Pid."

"My brother used to call me that," Ismail said. He looked down at the ground. "I used to follow them everywhere. Because I was the smallest, they said I was like a small rat following the bigger rats. I think I just miss being called that because I miss my brothers."

He paused, glancing over his shoulder at the Tower of Light.

I don't know what they'll do if they find out I'm passing the Golden Gates," he said, and he turned to face Nimra. "What about you, Nimra? What would your father say?"

"My father is dead," said Nimra. She looked away, south, toward the dark clouds and the gates on the horizon.

"What happened?" Ismail asked.

Nimra took a deep breath. Her hands clenched into fists.

"My father was put to death by King Idun for not following Prince Lovnor into the Middle-lands," she said. "He was labeled as a coward, but my father didn't believe in war. He didn't want it."

"What about your mother?" Ismail asked.

"I don't know. She ran away after my father died. My grandmother didn't tell me much, but she gave me my mother's wedding ring."

Nimra held out her hand so Ismail could see it. A pale blue metal band sat on one of her thin fingers. In its center, a white gem sparkled.

"I'm so sorry," said Ismail, but Nimra surprised him by smiling.

"Don't be," she said. "This was a long time ago. This was many moon-passes and many ages ago. But what about your mother? It's only fair now that you tell me about her."

"I really do not know anything about my mother," Ismail said slowly. "My father never speaks of her, and my own memories of her are few. My brothers aid she was really beautiful, and that she had an amazing voice, and that she liked to sing."

"She must have been a lovely person," Nimra said. "Do you know what happened to her?"

"No. None of my brothers know, but my father said his arrogance is to blame. I don't even know her name," Ismail said.

Above them, Laenatan hooted. Both Nimra and Ismail stood, shouldering their bags again, and started walking south.

Ismail looked back once at the Tower of Light glowing brightly.

"I miss my home," he said. "I wish I could say goodbye to my father."

"No," Nimra said firmly. "My grandmother said he would try to stop you from going on this quest."

"I know," Ismail said, and he turned south again.

"Give me the map, and I'll lead," said Nimra. She took the map and guided them forward, west and south, toward a mound of hills that Ismail guessed were full of caves. Above them, Laenatan circled almost lazily, blinking when the light from the tower pierced his eyes.

CHAPTER FOURTEEN – The Fate of Us

"Why me? Why?" Hassen kicked at the floor as he walked through the hopeless building toward the dungeons. Even on the upper levels, walls that were white were now dark with old blood.

Every few seconds, cries and screams of pain rang through the dark corridors. Hassen grew more worried as he meandered through the halls, searching for Ingie.

"He's in the dungeon," one soldier said when Hassen finally broke down and asked.

Hassen walked down several flights of narrow stairs. A long corridor stretched in front of him. To the sides, narrow cells were crammed with Norm prisoners, who were tied up and given no food or water. All they could do was wait for their turns to be tortured.

"Help me," a Norm prisoner begged as Hassen walked forward. Hassen ignored him and moved faster, hoping he wouldn't have to stay long in the dungeons.

"Help me. Help me. Help me."

With each step, it seemed as if another Norm prisoner begged Hassen's aid, but he kept walking. He didn't want to believe it was real, didn't want to see people having their limbs chopped off or being dragged around by their feet.

The Khad never visited the house of slaughter. Hassen's stomach turned as he passed another prisoner, who was sitting on the floor with both arms tied tightly above him. Hassen covered his eyes as he passed, but he still heard the prisoner's whispers.

"One survives. One dies. One survives. One dies."

A few steps further, Hassen entered the torture chamber, where Ingie was busy with a prisoner.

"Why are you down here?" Ingie demanded. "The Khad do not travel to the sign of death. You cowards are better off hiding."

The Norm he was torturing screamed as Ingie shoved him further down on a bed of nails.

"Please, stop!" the man cried. "I told you, I don't have a son."

"Shut it, or I'll push you further onto the table," Ingie said, as the jailers behind him laughed.

"St. Lawrence has a quest for us," said Hassen.

"Us?" said Ingie. "There's no us, you hear me?"

"I understand. The Saint has a quest for you."

"Does he? Let's go talk to him, then." Ingie set his hammer aside and turned to the jailers. "Keep pushing this scum down until he tells us where his son is," he said.

"Yes," one jailer said. "Would you like us to wait to kill him until you get back?"

"No. He won't have anything that would interest me," said Ingie, and he moved to the corridor, beckoning to Hassen. "You come with me, Khad spy. Now."

CHAPTER FIFTEEN –
The Northern Alliance

Traditions were apparent as the armies of the Qazams and northern Norms reached the Golden Gates.

The Qazams moved in a single line, and Prince Sumer lead his cavalry in complete sync with one another. Their long bows and pointed ears looked elegant in the tower's light.

In contrast, the northern Norms marched brutishly forward, pounding the ground with their feet without any rhythm. This swarm of warriors were led by the king himself.

When the oddly opposed armies reached the arches of the Golden Gates, they almost immediately started making fun of each other and bickering.

"What are you wearing?" A Norm asked a Qazam soldier, "And why do you have such pointed ears?"

"Why do you walk like a dog?" the Qazam replied.

"Oh, did your mother give you that dress?" the Norm asked. "Are you sure you're a boy? Why do you have flowers in your hair?"

King Duncan yelled at his armies. "Shut it!"

He trotted his horse between his men and the Qazam army, leading four of his oldest sons. They had never seen the High King's Road before, nor Qazams, but they were known to be witty. King Duncan hoped that they would become true leaders on this trip.

Suthen, the eldest prince, was the most driven to be a leader, but he was the one the king worried about most, too. Because he wanted power, he was the most susceptible to the curse of darkness in the south.

Under King Duncan's command, the Norms quieted, but the armies continued to size each other up.

The Norms were large in number and large in size. They carried big iron weapons, including chains with hooks, called palks, that could be used to rip away enemy flesh. They didn't carry shields or bows, preferring instead to fight like bears with nothing to lose.

The Qazam army was more disciplined, and Sumer lead them by strategy. They were all slim, quick on their feet and well-armed with long bows and two blades each on their backs.

The armies had one thing in common. None of them had ever seen the Middle-lands. In the north, they were constantly protected by the Golden Gates. Only a few of them suspected that this adventure would change life for all of them.

King Duncan and Prince Sumer greeted each other, and the two leaders rode up to the Golden Gates.

"Who goes there?" asked a watcher from the top of the wall.

"Duncan, King of the Norms." The Norms cheered and waved their weapons at the sound of his voice.

"Sumer, Prince of the Qazams." Unlike the Norms, the Qazam stood still, but pride filled their faces.

"How long are your travels in the Middle-lands, my Habibis?" asked the watcher from the wall.

Sumer looked at Duncan, who shouted up to the watchers.

"We were asked by the High King to aid his sons," he said. "We'll come back when they do."

"Ah," the watcher said. "Prince Umar said they would return in three moon-passes. You may leave through the Golden Gates. May you fear nothing but the Lord!"

"Open the arch!" a watcher yelled, and the chains of the gate started to rock. As the gates opened, bright light crept beneath them, illuminating the lands to the south. The armies started to march.

"Stay close to me, my young prince," Duncan said to Sumer. "You have never been to the Middle-lands, have you?"

Sumer appeared to be a little bit overwhelmed.

"No, this is the first time for me and for all of my men," he said.

"It's my first time past the arches, too," King Duncan said. "Come, young prince, our fates are ahead!"

CHAPTER SIXTEEN – The Calm Before the Storm

The night brought rain, more dark clouds, and an uneasy feeling. The people of Mik-Mag were used to this, but it was new for the young kin of the north. The soldiers camped for the night near the outskirts of the burned-out village.

To pass the time, some of the soldiers played a famous card game from the north called Tarneeb. Others played music on the instruments they brought with them, singing loudly as they smoked hookahs and drank chai.

For the princes, there was more work to be done. Once their big camp tent was set up, they brought in a table and held a council.

"This rain makes everything wet and muddy," Prince Kaf said. "Even with our kin here, it's hard to feel at home."

"We'll decide what to do tonight," Prince Umar said. "Once we have a course of action, we'll be able to fulfill our mission and get back home."

Their men were miserable. After a while, the songs and the warmth of the chai faded. They huddled in their tents, too damp and uncomfortable to sleep.

"I'm already missing home," Zuda said. "I wonder what my parents are doing right now without me. I have never been so far from home for this long. Am I the only one who feels this way?"

"I miss home, too, and I'm ready to go back," said Azui. "Why does this rain never stop?"

Azui was the youngest of the Northern Kin, and usually the most cheerful. The darkness and the rain were wearing him down.

"I don't know," a soldier named Gabe said. "It's been raining for days now. It's too wet to start a fire, and I feel like I'm getting sick." He stood, peeled back the tent flap and looked toward the tent where the princes were talking.

"Why are they still in there?" he said. "We need to move out of this place before something happens."

Zuda looked up. "What do you mean?"

"We're like sitting ducks," Gabe said. "This weather brings dark clouds. We've never even trained in elements like these before."

The men in the tent frowned at each other. As Gabe dropped the tent flap again, the young princes in the large tent discussed possible plans until the early hours of the morning.

"We are at Mik-Mag, as our O-Father wanted, but what now?" asked Kaf. He paced the tent, shivering as he remembered the vision he saw.

"Can you please sit down?" Adn said. He stretched out in a chair, but his eyes were haunted as he contemplated how the poor city was a shell of what it must have once been. "You're making me nervous. Here, smoke this hookah."

"How can we sit?" Kaf snapped, brushing the hookah aside angrily. "Do you see this city? Do you see these poor people? Do you see death everywhere you look? Because I do."

"What can we do about it now?" Adn asked. "We shouldn't be arguing about something that's already happened."

"He's right," Umar said. "We can't do anything about what happened here already, but we can prepare for whatever will happen next."

"Prepare for what? These people are not soldiers. They don't have armies. They do not even have weapons to protect themselves, except the old junk they sell to travelers," Kaf said.

"We are here to push back the darkness and anything that comes with it," said Umar. "That is exactly what we are going to do." His confidence slipped a little as he looked at his brothers, and questions filled both his eyes and his voice. "The people around here are hiding something," he said.

"We need to go into the city and start asking questions."

Kaf's anger stabbed into the dim light of the tent. "I remembered what O-Father said, and we shall push back this darkness, as we promised," he said. "I also agree that the people hide something from us, but we need more soldiers if we intend to stay here to protect them." He slammed his fist into the open palm of his other hand. "We only have 5,000 soldiers with us. All of them are young, and none of us are battle-ready."

"I agree." Adn leaned back in his chair, drew a breath on the hookah, and blew a big ring of smoke towards Kaf's head. "We need more soldiers, especially if we plan to ride south. We can ask the citizens of this city if they want to aid us. They have been hopeless for so long they might be happy to have the chance to fight back the evil that plagues them."

"That might be a good idea." Umar rubbed his chin with his hand, and his eyebrows raised with hope as the beginning of a plan took shape. "We could surely use their help, and they already have horses. We can give them the weapons they need."

Kaf nodded sharply, but he still looked tense. "Okay," he said. "I'll talk to the elders of the city tomorrow and see if they're willing to aid us."

Umar nodded his agreement. "Adn, stop smoking and go get the soldiers ready," he said. "We need to get ready to ride south past Mik-Mag."

"Yes, my brother," said Adn, and he left the tent to prepare the troops. Many of them, who couldn't sleep in their dripping tents, huddled under canopies around weak fires, shivering and forlorn. Some looked scared. All of them appeared exhausted, but they quieted their complaints as Adn drew near.

"All-right, men, get ready to ride," he said, hoping his voice carried more confidence than he felt. "We will be going to Mik-Mag to see if there are any citizens there who will join us as we ride south. You have until sunrise to prepare."

"Sunrise." Someone coughed behind his hand. "There is no sunrise here in this muddy, light-forsaken land."

Adn ignored him, brushed off the drops of water that slid down his golden attire, and walked briskly away toward where the horses were tethered.

"Why do we need the people of this city?" Zuda said, wrinkling his brow as he followed after Adn. "These people are not fighters. They have no battle warriors."

"You're right, but we are also no fighters," Adn said quietly. "We haven't fought in a battle yet."

Zuda nodded, catching Adn's foul mood, and decided to not tempt him with opposition. Behind them, the soldiers were murmuring as they rushed around, readying themselves for another uncomfortable ride.

"Yes," Zuda said quietly. "You might be right."

Umar emerged from the royal tent, already wearing his battle attire and his green gems. His black hair hung low around his strained face. He called to the hurried soldiers, and they gathered around him sullenly.

"As you know, we do not have many soldiers to fight back what might lie ahead us," he said. "I sent Kaf to talk to the elders in the city to see if anyone wants to join us as we ride south. We will fight back anything that brings danger to us. We will bring peace to the Middle-lands."

The soldiers quieted as Umar spoke to them, but their faces wore fear and worry.

"I warn you that I do not know what is past the city, but you must trust me as a leader," Umar said, and his voice rose with a false confidence. "Put your trust in me. I have sent a few soldiers southward to scout the lands and report back to me. They will return soon, and when they do, I will let you know exactly where we are going to ride. Now let's mount our horses and ride to the city. We will see if Kaf was successful in his petition, and if the elders of the city will grant our request for more men."

He clapped his hands, and the group of the soldiers broke apart, hurrying to pack the wet tents and saddle their horses. Some trembled nervously, but a few seemed unfazed, as if they didn't care about whatever evil might lie in the south.

"Do you really think the people city of Mik-Mag might join us?" Adn asked Umar.

"I do not know, but I have a bad feeling about what could happen if we do not get aid or soldiers," Umar replied.

"Now you are worrying me." Adn tried to laugh as he rode forward toward the city, but the sound was forced, and they both knew it. His mirth sounded as hollow and void of light as the muddy, rainy land.

"Prince Umar?" Azui trotted his horse up next to the princes, as he had many times before, but something in his countenance showed reluctance. He seemed to be afraid, as if his questions might anger them.

"Yes, Azui?" Umar lifted his chin, trying to show courage that he didn't feel.

"Why are we asking the Middle-land Norms for aid, and not our High King?" Azui's voice was low and nervous.

"I know you might be scared, Azui but we need the Norms of the Middle-lands to aid us now. The High King is too far away from us." Umar smiled affectionately, but his hands gripped the reins of his horse more tightly, whitening his knuckles. "I will send the High King a raven, if it will make you feel better."

Azui nodded. He tried to smile, but his face still appeared pinched and stressed.

"Thank you, Prince Umar," Azui said, and he nodded as he backed his horse away. Umar stared after him for a moment, suddenly feeling stifled, as if the darkness was a blanket over his head.

Few knew the curse of the darkness. Prince Umar was beginning to feel it, even if he didn't understand it.

Bitter Farewell

CHAPTER SEVENTEEN – Bitter Farewell, Part 2

"Here," whispered Nimra, as she and Ismail made their way towards a dim cave underneath the Golden Gates. They moved slowly, silently dodging the soldiers who patrolled the area. They crouched often in the shadows, as if they were frozen in place. They needed to avoid attracting the attention of the watchers.

"Slow down," Nimra told Ismail, pulling on the back of his sleeve. "You almost stumbled. I don't want anyone to hear us."

As they neared the mouth of the cave, Ismail noticed that bushes and long tree branches covered most of the entry to this old passage. Even in the light, it was difficult to see where the cave opened.

"It looks like no one has been here for ages," Ismail said uneasily.

"I know." Nimra whispered again. "It's dark in there. Did you bring any torches with you?" She peered into the entry as if she could decipher what lay inside the darkness.

Laenatan hooted as he flew down, landing on a tree branch next to Ismail, who was searching through his oversized bag.

"There's no turning back if we pass this cave," said Laenatan. "You know this, right, oath-keeper?"

Nimra turned her head, irritated. She couldn't understand Laenatan, but she knew he spoke to Ismail. Ismail seemed frustrated, too.

"Why didn't you tell me you used to be a boy from the Golden age?" Ismail didn't even look up as he rummaged through the bag.

"So, the candle-maidens told you, huh?" Laenatan hooted sorrowfully. "I was never proud of what I did, but they turned me into this bird. I will never again know how my family lives, nor will I have a normal life." His voice broke in despair, and even Nimra seemed to understand his hopelessness. Her eyes softened as she looked at the owl, and she lowered her chin.

"The candle-maidens said they could undo the curse if you help us," Ismail said, and at last he pulled a torch out of the bag. He handed it to Nimra as Laenatan bobbed his head upward in sudden excitement.

"They said that?"

"Yes," Ismail said, adjusting the contents of the bag and tying it closed. "I would not lie to you, Laenatan. I think it would be horrible to not know what happened to my family and to lose my childhood the way you did, so I can feel sorry for you."

Laenatan blinked, as if hearing his name shocked him.

"You are my only hope, Ismail," the owl hooted softly. "I make you this vow. I will aid you in your quest, and I will follow you to the end, if it suits you."

Ismail gazed into the owl's face. He nodded. Behind him, Nimra lit the torch. When she beckoned toward them, Ismail stepped toward the dark cave, making his way carefully around the wild bushes. Rather than flying over the Golden Gates, Laenatan hopped slowly behind them.

"I've never seen the Golden Gates this close before," said Nimra.

"It's been ages since I was here, too," said Ismail. "The gold seems lighter than it used to be, or at least lighter than I remember it."

They took their first steps into the entry. Nimra wrinkled her nose.

"It smells weird in here," she said.

"I smell it, too, but I can't see much," Ismail said. "Can you hold the light closer to the floor?"

Laenatan's big claws dug into the dirt, scraping and crunching something along the floor as he hopped behind them.

They moved slowly. The light from the torch cast strange shadows in orange light on the cave walls and ceiling, but the floor below remained in darkness. Objects rolled under their feet as they walked toward the other side of the cavern, where the path toward the western land began.

Ismail slipped as he stepped on something hard, and Laenatan's eyes grew wide. Ismail froze as Laenatan, who still carried the heart of a boy in his large owl body, screeched.

"Hey, are those bodies?"

Chills ran over Ismail's scalp and down his back. "Skeletons," said Ismail, stumbling again over the bones of the long-dead. "Why are they here? Why?"

"Stop," said Nimra, bringing the torch toward the ground. "Don't move." She took a sharp breath. "It looks as if their eyes were covered."

Ismail knelt to get a closer look. "Yes. There are black cloths around the faces. This one looks like the cloth from an elder watcher." He poked the cloth gingerly as he stood again. Sorrow washed over him. "These are dead watchers from the top of the wall," he said. He took a few steps backward, realizing he had never seen this much death before.

"Let's go," Nimra whispered, and even though her voice was quiet, her breath quivered. They stepped around the edges of the dark cave, but even here their path was strewn with old bones. Some crushed as they stepped on them, powdering in to a light gray dust. They covered their mouths and noses with their hands and pushed forward.

"I see something," Nimra said. She pointed the torch toward the distant wall. As they moved toward it, the light from their torch was suddenly overpowered by a bright light that lit the entire cave with a flash.

"My son!" High King Alm's voice echoed in the bright cave.

Ismail, shocked and startled to see his father here, in this forgotten place, shouted his surprise. "O-Father!"

Both Nimra and Laenatan stood frozen in place. Their eyes flickered between the bright light of the High King in his golden attire and his watchful lion, Amir.

"Why, are you here, my son? You ran to the King's Wood, and now I find you in the under-path of the Golden Gates?" He glanced around the cave, noted the dead bodies, and moved forward, hoping to spare his son pain from the death he saw here.

Ismail noticed, and he swallowed. "O-Father, why are there dead watchers here?" He didn't mean to cry, but his eyes watered, and he wiped away the tears with the back of his hand.

"The Norms do not live as long our kin, my son, but even in death, the watchers are always at the wall, high and even low." Alm's own eyes watered, and Amir pawed through the skeletons, peering at Laenatan with curiosity. Laenatan hopped a little further behind Ismail but Nimra was still too shocked at the appearance of the High King to move.

Ismail tried to speak.

"I....I was...," he took a breath and turned toward Nimra and Laenatan. "Please, can you go ahead?"

Nimra didn't hesitate. She nodded and moved toward the light she had seen in the distance, away from the High King's soft glow. Laenatan hopped slowly behind her.

"Who are your new friends?" said Alm, and his face looked sad, as if he already knew what Ismail would say.

"I got lost in the High King's Woods," Ismail said. "I found a few monks. One of them said he spoke to you, while you were a boy."

Ismail looked up at his father, but Alm turned his face away, stricken. Tears slid down both of their cheeks.

"Who was the monk?" the High King asked, and his voice sounded broken.

"Sarvajna," Ismail said. "He passed away while I was speaking to him."

"You spoke to Sarvajna at Haeinsa tower?" The High King seemed shocked out of his sorrow, and then a darkness in him started to grow, diminishing his natural glow. Amir stepped to the side uneasily.

"What happened next?" King Alm asked. He spoke softly, but his voice trembled with rage.

Even Ismail felt the change in his father's tone. He had rarely seen his father angry. When he had, it had been a fearsome thing, but the truth was the only thing that could be spoken now.

"I met them," Ismail said.

"Them?" King Alm asked. "The candle-maidens?"

Ismail nodded. "They told me I need to take this quest and fight back the darkness that is coming."

King Alm's face pinched bitterly, and he spoke so quickly and loudly that spittle flew from his lips. "Those old hags are trying to take my last son from me?"

Ismail reached out, laying a hand on his father's arm to calm him. "No, O-Father. You failed in your quest," he said. "They told me a darkness is growing in the south and that I need to go see the Dragon King."

King Alm shook as he heard his youngest son's words, and as he remembered his own failure.

"I can't let you go, my son," he said. "Not now, not when Umar and Adn and Kaf are already gone. You are the only one left. I can let you leave, as well." He looked down into Ismail's steadfast face, remembering the horror he had seen in the Middle-lands during the Golden Age. He pleaded with his son. "Please. Stay."

"So, it's true," Ismail said. "My brothers are already in the Middle-lands. I was curious about why you left me at the cabin with Uncle Adu."

The High King placed his hands upon Ismail's shoulders, hoping to say more, but Ismail's next words stopped him.

"I must go, O-Father, lest this curse swallow us whole...as it has so many others," Ismail said, repeating the words of the candle-maidens.

After a long moment, King Alm spoke again. "It seems your fate is sealed," he said sadly. "I never thought this day would come. Why are the fates so cruel to us?"

He blinked, and the darkness in him dissipated. "This darkness is a curse. They say a true king can harness the curse. It is a lie, but I knew not better."

They stood in the cave for a long, quiet moment, ignoring the skeletons, the black cloths and even the light emanating from the High King. When he spoke again, his voice was gruff, but his manner was gentle.

"You have my aid, my son, if you take this quest. I will send help in any way that I can." He blinked, as if suddenly remembering something, and pulled a small glass bottle with a red cap from his vesture. Inside the bottle was a butterfly made of white light.

"Here. Take this. Wear it on your person at all times," said King Alm.

"What is this?" Ismail peered through the glass, amazed at the butterfly's beauty.

"This is an aldwa-farasha, a bright butterfly," King Alm said. "Wear it by your chest. This will fight back the darkness and the curse it can leave upon your heart. Listen to me, my son. The clouds that spread throughout the Middle-lands aren't normal clouds. They block the sun, but they also carry a curse that can spread through you like a virus. This aldwa-farasha will protect you from that."

As Ismail closed his hands around the bottle and slipped it inside his shirt, next to his chest, King Alm's voice grew more urgent. "You need to know this, my son," he said. "In my young age, I spent too much time in the darkness of the Middle-lands. You see, it's not just a cloud or a storm, but a person..."

"A person?" Ismail blinked and looked up sharply.

"Oh yes, my son. Do you think this darkness rises alone? No, but Ibies—the cursed one—he brings this darkness, this terrible curse that causes despair in the hearts of men such as me."

"What do you mean, O-Father? How are you affected?" Ismail sounded worried.

"You see, my son, if you spend too much of your life in the dark cloud, you lose yourself. If I did not have the tower of light and its glow, I would be lost. So would the land of Amer. I was afraid of this, and I shielded our kingdom from the south and other lands. I was only trying to protect us, but this darkness is growing faster than before."

He looked down at Ismail, and his face twisted in agony. "My son, you need to go. Go to the Castle of Blayney, and my aid will not be far away."

"My O-Father!" Ismail reached over the dead bodies and embraced the High King. "I don't know when or if I will see you again! They hugged quietly and long. Neither could speak. Finally, the High King pulled away and patted his son on the shoulders. His face was wet with tears.

"Go now, my son. Remember, we fear naught but the Lord."

Ismail reached into his pack, pulled out the rusted crown of the oath-keeper, and placed it on his head as his father watched. Then he shouldered the heavy bag and walked toward the dim light at the far side of the room, where Nimra and Laenatan waited for him. Once, he looked over his shoulder at his father, wondering how the High King knew he was going to the Castle of Blayney. He hadn't told him.

King Alm watched as Ismail reached Nimra and Laenatan. In a moment, the flicker of their torch had disappeared into the passageway that lay beyond.

"What will their fate be?" he whispered, and then he fell onto the ground full of skeletons. The despair of the curse overtook him, and the light of his glow dimmed as the tears flowed freely again.

"They say a true king can harness the curse," he cried. "It is but a lie, but I knew no better. I tried to conquer the dark, but I only fell into it."

He turned toward Amir, whose enormous golden paw rested on the ground beside him. "I failed them, Amir. I failed them all. I promised my people that I would save the land from the cursed one, but things only grew worse, and now I have lost all my sons for it. Am I a king or a pawn of fate?"

Amir shifted. He looked into King Alm's face, trying to find the right words, but the High King was already speaking again.

"I feel that I am losing my sanity. Take me back to the tower of light."

He reached out, touched Amir's golden fir, and climbed weakly onto the lion's back. Amir turned, took a few steps toward the cavern's entrance, and bounded twice over the bodies lying on the floor. As he exited the cavern, carrying the High King on his back, the cave filled with darkness once again.

CHAPTER EIGHTEEN – The Bitter Spiders

The two red eyes of Ibies watched as Ingie and Hassen reach the chamber of Saint Lawrence. Ingie rapped on the door quickly with the back of his knuckles, eager to get inside and tell the saint how he felt about working with Hassen.

"Come in," Saint Lawrence said softly.

Hassen folded his arms and leaned against the doorframe. "I'm going to stay out here."

"You sicken me," Ingie said. He walked in and closed the door behind him, but Hassen could easily hear the conversation beyond it.

"What do you want, Ingie?" Saint Lawrence said. He didn't look up from the note he was writing. Ingie glanced around at the books, notes and seals all over the floor as screams from the dungeons below filled the air.

"That coward said you want us to ride to the city of Mik-Mag. Why would we do that?"

"He's not mistaken. You take him, since he knows the area, and lead a small group of Asward soldiers.

"You want the Asward to ride to the city? They will tear that place apart!" Ingie's mouth fell open as he remembered the brutality of the Asward soldiers.

"Yes. Do not make me repeat myself, and go ride to the city. I will come behind with the rest of the Asward soldiers and the Ragrok beast." Saint Lawrence spoke calmly, and Ingie shuddered in spite of himself.

"You are mad to release that beast, thinking it will aid you," said Ingie. The cleanup would be never-ending. "Ever since Ibies appointed you here, you have been a thorn in my side."

Saint Lawrence swiveled on his chair, and although he spoke softly, Ingie heard the cold edge of violent rage in his voice. "You leave this room and ride to the city, or I will have you taken to the depth of this prison," the Saint said.

Ingie glared into Saint Lawrence's face, but he knew that this man was one of a few people who could turn his life to hell. He couldn't change his fate now. Instead, he turned abruptly and stomped out of the room.

"You come with me now," said Ingie, as he passed Hassen.

Behind them, the Saint had moved to the open door, and he chuckled as he watched them walk down the hall. "Have fun now," he called after them.

Once they were out of the earshot of the Saint, Ingie took his anger out on Hassen. "I blame you for this," he hissed. "You know, if you did not show up here, if you had just gone to the south, we wouldn't be going to war in the city."

"You think that I thought this would happen? I did not want to ride to Mik-Mag for a fight." Hassen spoke with bravado, but Ingie was well -seasoned, and he caught the break of fear in Hassen's voice.

"You have no choice now, spy," Ingie said. "You will come with me and a few of the Asward."

"The Asward?" Hassen almost gasped. "Are you serious? Those mad-men will destroy the entire city."

They left the dim tower to rally the troops. They stared at each other as they realized that they were both unwilling puppets.

Unfortunately, this common ground wasn't the sort of thing to build a friendship or even an alliance around. Ingie shouted at the soldiers he was in charge of.

"Listen up, boys," he said. "We have a new task from Saint Lawrence. He wants us to ride to the city of Mik-Mag. We will be aided by Asward soldiers."

He let that sink in, and when his men began to murmur, he shouted to get their attention again. "You know the asward are worst kind of soldiers and the worst kind of men, but their brutality is what we need. Get ready and we'll ride to the Asward camp."

"Why do you talk to them as if they have a choice?" Saint Lawrence, who had followed them, now stood at the top of the stairs near the tower entry. "None of you have a choice. Get going. Ride now, or you will all die."

The men hurried. Someone brought Ingie and Hassen their horses, and they mounted and rode off toward the Asward camp with only a few hundred soldiers. They were dark-armored and fearsome, with stained teeth and rusted swords, but they grew quiet as they rode. Saint Lawrence had sent a raven ahead of them. Even so, none of them knew how they would be received by the Asward soldiers.

The road in front of them was clear, except for occasional body parts as they drew close to the camp. When the sounds of big spiders running through the camp and the noisy screams of Middle-land Norms being tortured became clear, Ingie slowed his horse to a walk, and his men fell in behind him. Their faces were grim.

Even the soldiers of the saints stayed away from Asward camps. The Asward rode on enormous spiders who were bred only to kill and maim people. The spiders were feared even in the armies of Ibies. Only the Asward soldiers, who were the beloved troops of Ibies, had been given the power to understand and ride the spiders from the Widow Woods. Others would be ripped apart if they tried.

As they reached the outskirts of the camp, a voice called down from the top of the gate.

"Ingie, it's good you are here. Saint Lawrence said you would come. My soldiers are mounted and ready to head out."

"Sieg, we meet again," Ingie replied. "If you are ready, we should ride out right away. Saint Lawrence is already on edge."

"As you wish," Sieg said. He turned over his shoulder and yelled. "Open the gate!"

Heavy iron creaked as the gates opened, and Hassen shuddered as the strange sound of spiders breathing in long huffs filled his ears. These spiders had legs with knife-sharp ridges and spikes that could rip flesh from anyone that got too close. Their many eyes filled the tops of their heads, and a long red strip ran from their eyes all the way to the rear of their bodies.

Men clothed in black armor sat atop the spiders. Most carried two swords, and a few had spears, as well.

Sieg shouted again, and the Asward soldiers moved forward.

"Is this all?" said Ingie. "I only see about twenty Asward."

"Yes, the Saint wants my other soldiers to accompany him on his own ride to the city," said Sieg, "But these men should still be enough to help you. I trained them myself." He laughed, but the sound was humorless and rough.

Ingie and Hassen looked at each other. Doubt filled their faces, but then Ingie glared again.

"Alright," he said, shouting to his men. "You all know what the task is. We get to the city and get those bastard princes. It's that simple. Do you know how many soldiers the princes have, Hassen?"

Hassen paled. "Um, well I only met one prince, but I saw a lot of soldiers. They were all young, and none of them were fighters, if you ask me."

Ingie's temper rose. "You did not see the full cavalry?"

"I rode right to the tower of the Saint when I saw them," Hassen said. "I did not stop to count how many—"

"You're a coward. You know that, right?" Ingie turned his back on Hassen and waived his soldiers forward. "Let's ride!"

It was a two-day journey to the city of Mik-Mag. The Soldiers of the Saint and the Asward riders rode without stopping. Overhead, the dark clouds rippled and roiled, as if they accompanied the fearsome army.

Widow Woods

CHAPTER NINETEEN – The Widow Woods

Ismail, Nimra and Laenatan stood in wonder at the mouth of the cave on the south side of the wall, where the cave path emerged into the Middle-lands. Here the light of the north still permeated the air around them, even in spite of the shadow of the wall. However, when they looked southward, the clouds grew thicker and the land below it was too dark to be seen clearly.

"We have to go into that," Ismail said, and together they took their first steps forward. The certainty of a sealed fate combined with uneasy feelings about what the West-lands might hold for them. As they made their way toward the Castle of Blayney, the light behind them slowly faded away. Before long, they reached the edge of a forest. Ismail looked back at the Golden Gates, then forward into the trees.

"We have no idea what's ahead," he said. "Laenatan, fly in front let us know if you see anything. We'll be right behind you."

Laenatan nodded. "Okay, but Ismail, heed my warning. Do not trust anyone besides Nimra. We do not know who are our friends or foes. These woods are dark, and I won't be able to see you from the sky. I won't be able to help you at all."

"I understand," Ismail said. Although he felt uneasy, he and Nimra headed into the woods as Laenatan took to the sky. With every step they took, the leaves on the trees looked less green. They took on a sickly brown color.

"I will see you on the other side of the woods!" Laenatan called.

He was barely out of sight when Nimra spoke.

"Are you going to tell me what your father said?"

Ismail tried to ignore the sickness in the trees, and talking seemed like a good distraction.

"He seemed broken," Ismail said. "I have never seen my O-Father like this. Something inside him has become unstable."

"I swear I thought he would take you back to the Tower of Light," Nimra said. "Why do you think he let you go, when he knows that you might die?"

"Die?" Ismail frowned. "I did not think I would die, but I'm sure that deep inside he knew this day would come. He knew we were going to the Castle of Blayney, even though I didn't tell him so."

"That's interesting," Nimra said. "It seems like he planned for you to meet with the candle-maidens. My grandmother told me he stopped by a few times, a long time ago, but she never told me why."

They stepped around moldy or shriveled roots. The woods were thick here, and the long branches were bare in patches. In some places, twigs had fallen from the trees, and when Ismail or Nimra stepped on them, they were dry and brittle.

"These woods are dying," Nimra said. "This place looks like a planet that has never seen the light."

"I know what you mean," Ismail said. "It's creepy here. We need to head straight and find our way out."

"Out?" Nimra peered ahead, but there were too many tree trunks to see far. Her brow furrowed. "I don't see a way out of this forest. We'll have to keep going for a while."

There wasn't much to talk about now, but when they weren't conversing, the forest was eerily silent. When they looked up, they occasionally saw the sky, but the light from the tower had faded completely.

"Is it getting darker?" Ismail asked. "I feel like something is coming."

"The sun's rays are being blocked by the branches of the trees," Nimra said. "We need to walk carefully." She pulled out the torch Ismail gave her in the cave, but she hesitated before she lit it.

"Ismail, do you think we should light the torch? Something might catch fire. So many of the trees are dead, and the leaves are all dry, but we can't see anything. Do we even have a choice?"

"I have no idea about that, but what is causing the death in the trees might be here with us." Ismail shifted uneasily and glanced around him. "We need to get out of these woods fast."

Nimra nodded. "Let's use the torch, then. It can help us find our way out of these deep woods."

She lit the torch, and they moved forward quickly, but the torch only provided enough light to see a little more of their surroundings.

"Webs!" Nimra gasped. "Do you see those webs on the trees?"

She leaned a bit closer to a tree that was covered with large, white, sticky webs. She held the torch higher, following the web strands as they connected two trees together. "We could have walked right into this, and we would have been stuck," she said.

"We should burn the webs and get through," Ismail said, and he took the torch from Nimra's hand.

"Are you sure?" She asked. "Those are big webs. They must have been built by something pretty big." She wrapped her arms around her sides, as if the uneasy feeling within was becoming too much to bear.

"Don't worry," Ismail said. "We need to get past this to get out of the woods. This is the quickest way to move straight forward."

He held the torch up so that the flames began to singe the strands.

"No," wailed a voice from the tree. It was a loud, long sound, but it was also mournful. Ismail jumped, almost dropping the torch, and turned to look at Nimra.

"Did you hear that?" he asked.

Nimra looked confused. "Hear what?"

"You did not hear a loud 'no' in a high-pitched voice?" He turned around again and held the flames to the edge of the web in front of him.

"No!" A black spider the size of a cat lunged forward on a low-hanging branch, far enough into the torchlight that Ismail could see three red dots on its head. "Stop that!" the spider said.

"What is that!" Nimra jumped back, drew her bow, and aimed an arrow at the spider's head.

"Stop!" Ismail stepped in front of her.

"Why? It's disgusting!" she said.

"Oh, really, she's not wrong," said the spider.

This caused Ismail to turn around again. "What are you?" he asked.

"You can understand me?" The spider rose higher on its legs, as if it felt as surprised as Ismail and Nimra. "That's interesting." The spider made a strange huffing sound that could have been a laugh.

The spider was as creepy as it was large. Big eyes jutted out from its head, and its legs were long and spiky.

"Who are you? What are you? Why can I understand you?" Ismail asked.

"Oh, you must be Northern Kin," the spider said. "I see. Interesting. You look reasonably sane, so what are you doing in these woods?"

Two of the spider's legs rose to his sides, and two of its fangs, as it stifled another strange, huffing laugh. "Are you lost or something?" the spider asked. "May I help you find your way?"

Nimra looked at Ismail, at the spider, and Ismail again. Confusion filled her face. Ismail was clearly speaking with the spider, but all she heard was gibberish.

"You know the way out, but why would you help us?" Ismail asked the spider.

"I'm just a helpful spider, willing to aid anyone in need—especially Northern Kin," said the spider. He jumped to the forest floor and crawled toward Ismail.

"Helpful and willing," Ismail said. "You're too witty. Perhaps you have your own agenda. May I ask your name?"

The spider laughed again. "I'm Igor, the helpful spider. I'm probably the only helpful spider in these woods."

"How long have you been here?"

"My kind has lived in these woods for hundreds of years, but we rarely see Northern Kin," the spider said. He seemed to be assessing Ismail as he spoke. "A few other tribes have come and gone, just like the animals. Only we stay in this dark forest."

"Igor, I've never met an Igor before—I mean, I've never seen a spider before," said Ismail.

"I'm happy to be your first," the spider laughed. "May I ask who you are, and who your blonde friend is?" It was hard to tell, but it seemed to Ismail that the spider's voice grew more sinister.

Ismail didn't trust this spider, and he didn't want to give him his real name. "I'm Augo, and that's my sister, Nimra," he said.

"So why are you here in these dark woods?" Igor asked. "If you take the wrong steps, you could be greatly harmed. Beasts and ghosts live here. Old rituals take place here, too. It's blood for blood. You must stay with me. I'll show you the right path."

"What do you mean, beasts and ghosts? My O-Father said all the ancient beasts were dead. They died during the Golden Age." Ismail's tone grew more distrustful as he spoke, and he took a half-step back, away from the spider. "Why do you want so badly to help us? What are your intentions?"

"Intentions? I have no intentions. I just want to help two kids who got lost in these dark woods." Igor straightened and stared Ismail in the face. "Your father does not know these woods as well as he thinks he does," the spider said. "Beasts still live in these woods. They grow slowly, but they are becoming uncontrollable even now. As the days grow darker, so do their intentions."

Nimra cleared her throat. "What's he saying?" she whispered.

"He said he'll help us get out these woods," Ismail said. "What do you think?"

"You can understand this little tick," said Nimra, "But that doesn't mean anything. I'm not sure we should trust this creature of the night."

"His name is Igor," said Ismail. "He's kind of...different."

"Tell her I'm not a tick," said Igor.

"I don't trust it," said Nimra. She stepped to the side, still holding her bow and arrow, still ready to fire. "I don't think we have much of a choice, though."

Ismail turned back to Igor. "You can assist us out of these woods, but Igor, if you try anything, we'll defend ourselves," he said. He stared straight into Igor's many bulging eyes.

Igor huffed his laughter again and rubbed two of his feet together. "Good, good," he said. "Come with me. This way. We'll find the right path soon."

As Nimra and Ismail followed the spider, they whispered.

"It doesn't feel like we're going straight anymore, does it?" Nimra said.

"No," Ismail replied. "I don't think he's leading us to the right path. He may be trying to trap us, so keep your guard up."

"Come, young ones," Igor laughed, and as he scurried along the forest floor, he babbled on. "You wear the amazing attire of Northern Kin," he said. "You must be special to have such fine gems on you. I've never seen gems this beautiful in all my years in this forest. Are you sure you're lost?"

"Yes," Ismail said. "We got separated from our family, and we will surely pay you once we get out of these depressing woods."

"What? You lied?" Nimra whispered, but before she could say more, Ismail whispered back to her. "I'm trying not to give him too much information," he said.

"Yes, yes," Igor said loudly. "These woods are really dark. Legends say a curse has come to these lands, which is something that only we spiders can benefit from. The deer and the rabbits can no longer live here, but we do."

"We haven't seen any other spiders," Ismail said.

Igor raced around the root of a tree. "My kind is leaving the forest," he said. "We spiders are spreading far into the Middle-lands now. By the way, did you know I have a liking for bright gems? I would love to have your gems as a payment…when we reach your family, that is."

Ismail looked at Nimra, not sure what to say, but she didn't understand the conversation, and she couldn't help him.

"Sure. Once we make it out of these woods, you shall have these gems," Ismail said.

"Excellent! Come this way!" Igor scurried faster, and Ismail and Nimra had to pick up their pace to keep up.

"Where is he going?" said Nimra, finally slinging her arrow back into its quiver and shouldering her bow. "It's getting darker, and the trees appear more dead than those we passed earlier."

"This way," said Igor. He zipped into a dark cave.

"We can't go in there," said Ismail. He stopped, and Nimra stood beside him.

"If you want to get home, come this way." Igor hopped out of the cave, waiving toward it with one of his legs. "It's a short passage that will lead you out of these woods. I promise."

"We'll take action if you try to trick us," Ismail said, and he stepped forward again.

Igor laughed. "No action will be needed, young Northern Kin. Come this way."

Inside the cave, the light from Ismail's torch barely reached their feet. The cave was filled with boulders and gaping holes, so Ismail and Nimra had to move carefully. Igor, on the other hand, dashed ahead.

"Slow down!" Ismail called, but Igor, still laughing, had disappeared from sight.

"Igor, where are you?" Ismail called. "Igor!"

The light from Ismail's torch fell toward their feet as they moved into another cavernous area. The bones of animals lay scattered across the floor.

"He led us to a trap!" Nimra cried.

"You are both fools," Igor laughed, hiding in the shadows beyond the torchlight.

"You betray us," Ismail said. "My Abu always said never trust a spider, not even a small tick like you."

"You shall die here, and I will have your golden attire," Igor said. "I shall eat both of you. I look forward to drinking your blood."

Igor's voice echoed as he shifted, sneaking through the darkness.

"You will not have us, Igor," said Ismail. "You are one spider, and a small one, at that. You speak of beasts and ghosts, but the only beast I know is a small tick."

The taunts got to Igor. "I'm not small! How dare you?" he squealed as he ran out of the corner. He attacked Ismail.

"Ouch!" said Ismail, looking down as Igor bit his leg. Ismail pulled out his sword and swung it at Igor again and again. He didn't hold back, even tossing the torch aside in order to fight Igor more effectively.

"You bring us here to die!" said Ismail, swinging his blade quickly at Igor. It connected with one of Igor's legs, slashing it open. Purple blood gushed from the wound.

"You cut my leg!" Igor screamed.

"I promised you, you creature of the night, so if you want to die, keep coming at us!"

Igor hissed and ran forward again. In spite of his injured leg, he leapt at Ismail's face. Ismail dodged out of the way, but both Ismail and Nimra stumbled backward. They fell off a cliff near the back of the cave.

"Ahh!" Ismail and Nimra yelled as they fell. Their bodies thudded as they landed hard on the sand floor of the cave.

Above them, clinging to the rocks of the cliff, Igor watched his foes fall. Once again, he laughed. "You shall die here. I shall come back and take all your gems. I shall! I shall! It was good doing business with you!"

For Ismail, getting the wind knocked out of him from the fall was nothing compared to the dismal sound of Igor's uncontrollable laughter. He glared up at the spider, but Nimra was more important. She whimpered, and he sat up, scuttled to her and tried to catch his breath.

"Are you okay?" he asked.

"I think so," she said, struggling to sit up. "Yes, I'm fine. But why did he attack us?"

"He led us here to die," Ismail said. "He wants to rob us of our gems and my rusted crown. He attacked me, and I only protected us."

"This whole week has been crazy," Nimra said. "First there's a tall owl only you can talk to, then the bones of the watchers, and meeting your father looking like this, and now a little tick spider tricked us. What do we do now?"

"We need light," Ismail said. "We need another torch."

He rummaged in his pack, still talking to Nimra. "That tick almost killed us. I wish I knew why I can understand these creatures. It's been happening ever since I met that monk in the High King's forest. It seems odd to me, too. Aha, I got one!"

As he pulled out a torch and handed it to Nimra, they both heard a voice in the distance.

"Hello?"

"Who's that?" Nimra whispered, and she and Ismail exchanged worried looks.

"Did you hear the voice that time?" Ismail asked.

"Yes!"

"I hope this isn't a ghost," Ismail said. "Igor told me there are ghosts in these woods."

"A ghost? You didn't fill me in on that part, while you and that tick giggled and chatted it up back there!"

"Yes, he said ghosts and beasts fill these woods," Ismail said. "Let's not talk about this right now!"

"Hello," a voice in the distance said again.

"You should go take a look," said Ismail.

"Why me?" Nimra shot back. "I don't want to go."

As they argued in whispers, they heard the repeating words of a mumbling voice.

"Who am I? Why? No, no, no!"

"Okay, we both go together," Nimra said, finally lighting the torch.

"You lead," said Ismail. He walked behind Nimra, using her as a shield as they made their way toward the odd voice.

"What's it saying?" asked Nimra as they drew closer.

"I don't know, but I'm not having my guard down again," said Ismail. He pulled out his sword.

The light from the torch fell on the figure of an old woman in a torn white dress. Blood stains splattered the once beautiful cloth. Her long, unkempt hair was gray and dull.

"It's not a ghost," Nimra and Ismail said at the same time, and then Nimra gasped.

"Oh, who are you?" she said. She stared at the old lady with wide eyes.

"Who am I? I don't know," the old woman said. "This darkness is a curse. I can't remember anything through the darkness."

"Do you know your name?" asked Ismail.

"I had a name, once, but I don't remember it now," said the lady. "My memories have faded away."

Nimra, still wide-eyed, drew closer to the old woman. She reached out and touched her gray hair, pulling it back to reveal her pointed ears.

"Mother? Mother, what are you doing in this horrible place?"

Ismail's shock echoed Nimra's. "That's your mother?"

"Mother," the old woman said. "I'm not your mother."

"Mother, it's me, Nimra! Don't you remember?" Nimra's shock turned to a panicked flood of tears, and she fell to her knees. "It's Nimra! I'm your daughter, remember?"

The old lady grew agitated, then angry, and she pulled away. "I don't have a daughter!" she yelled.

"It's okay," said Ismail, taking the torch from Nimra's shaking hands while she sobbed. "It's okay."

He patted Nimra's shoulder awkwardly as he spoke to the old woman.

"We got lost and fell from that cliff up above," he said. "Do you know how to get out of here?"

"There's no getting out," the woman said. "You will be stuck in this darkness and lose yourself, just as I did. I have been here for longer than I can remember, but why? Why am I here?"

She began muttering again, and Ismail gave Nimra's shoulder a squeeze. "Are you okay?"

"I cannot believe she's here," Nimra said. "Why is she here, and why doesn't she remember me?"

"She seems to have been here for quite a while," Ismail said. Nimra's sobs slowed, and she hiccupped as she caught her breath. He grabbed her hand and pulled her to her feet. "Help me look around this area," he said. "It's too dark to explore on my own."

They walked around the room, feeling the walls, the boulders and occasionally the bones of others who had fallen into the spider's trap. The air smelled of dust, and there was no sense of time, but the despair settled on everything. Their urgency to get out, to escape, was dire.

"How do you think she got here?" Nimra asked, glancing through the dark toward her mother. "Why is she here?"

"I hope that spider didn't have anything to do with this," said Ismail. "I knew I shouldn't have trusted him."

"That spider! We can ask her if she saw it," Nimra said. "Maybe that's how she got stuck here."

Ismail stumbled over something. He reached down and pulled a small leather bag from the floor. "Look what I found!"

He opened the bag and pulled out a candle and a book filled with Qazam writing. He handed them to Nimra.

Grandmother said my mother was tasked to go to the Castle of Blayney," said Nimra. "So that's it! She was coming here, just like us, and got lost, just like us."

"Do you think she will remember anything if she looks at these things?" asked Ismail. He handed the bag to Nimra. "Take them to her and she if she can remember anything."

Nimra nodded. She walked toward her mother quietly, slowly, as if every footfall would break through her mother's fragile reverie and bring back her anger.

"Hey," Nimra said. She placed the bag close to her mother and laid the items out on top. "We found your bag. Do you remember any of these things? The candle? Maybe this book, with your name on it?"

She lifted the book and held it closer to her mother.

"That ring," said the woman. "That ring on your finger."

"Oh, do you know this ring?" asked Nimra.

"Ah. my memory is fading, but that ring—I remember it, but I do not know how or why."

"It's yours," Nimra said. "This ring is yours. Father gave it to you on your wedding day. Do you remember? She looked upon her mother, who was aging quickly, but her love was still strong.

"I don't know," said the lady.

"Here." Nimra pulled the ring from her finger. Tears slid down her cheeks again. "Take it. It's yours."

"No, Honey. You keep it," said the lady.

Nimra sniffled and wiped a tear from her face as she stared at the shell of her mother. Something broke through her mother's vague memory, and for an instant, she seemed to recognize Nimra—but it faded too quickly for Nimra to be sure.

"I do not remember who you are," the woman said. "If you're right, if I am your mother, then please forget who I was and move on. Please. I can only bring more harm to you, because this darkness is a curse that has spread through me so that I slowly lose who I am."

"She's right," Ismail said. "Something is terribly wrong with this place. We need to find a way out."

"I cannot leave her here," said Nimra, and her voice broke again.

"Go, child," the woman said. "Do not let me hold you back. Go be who you can be. I will be no help to you. I can only be a burden."

"You won't be a burden, mother!" Nimra cried. "Please come with us! We will find help for you. Maybe we can take you back to the north. Maybe the High King can help you!"

Ismail spoke up, sadly but firmly. "No. We cannot go back, Nimra. We must push forward to the Castle of Blayney like your grandmother said. As the oath-keeper, I say we must keep going."

"Listen to your friend, and leave this forgotten place, lest this curse take you, as it has so many others," said the woman. Nimra could bear it no longer. She reached for a hug, but her mother sat still, not moving, as if she were a dead body.

"I love you, Mother" said Nimra. Her tears fell into the gray strands of her mother's hair.

"I know." The woman's voice was sad but flat, and the vagueness covered her eyes again.

"Come, Nimra," said Ismail as he gathered his items and repacked his oversized bag. "Let's find a way out. We can start in the corner where we found that bag. I think I heard some wind there. That might be a good place to start."

"Okay," Nimra said, standing slowly. Just give me a few seconds. I want to say one more goodbye." She reached out and touched her mother's face. "Mother, I love you, and I really hope you will come with us. Please," Nimra begged.

The lady mumbled again. "Who, who am I? Why? No, no, no, please, don't."

Nimra withdrew her hand. She looked once more on her mother and slowly walked away with Ismail, trying to ignore her mother's words.

"Why? Why can I not remember?"

"We need to go," Ismail said. "I know this is hurting you, but we cannot end up like her. You have to let this go."

"I know, but I feel like this will kill me," said Nimra.

They reached the corner where they found the bag. The torch only provided a few feet of light, but the light sound of air flow caught their attention.

"Do you hear that?" asked Ismail. He crouched close to the wall.

"I hear wind," said Nimra.

"Let's put the torch here," Ismail said. "Maybe we can dig our way out from this wall. If we can hear wind, it must be weak."

They scooped sand, rock, gravel and clay with their hands, pulling it away from a section of wall that was made mostly of clay. It broke easily, but they were only able to make a small hole. They could squeeze through, one at a time, but it would be tight.

"Do you think we can make this hole bigger, for her?" asked Nimra.

"She would not listen to us!" said Ismail. "She's already repeating the same line she said once we first met her."

Nimra nodded, but her expression was bitter. "You go first through the hole," she said.

Ismail climbed into the hole and moved through it—first his head, then his shoulders, and then his waist. "I see a tree. I think it is safe," he yelled, and he pulled his legs through the hole.

"I'm coming," said Nimra. She looked back at her mother one last time. The old woman sat in a corner of the dark area, mumbling to herself, trying to hold onto any memory she could find. Nimra looked away and pushed herself into the tight opening. As she crawled through, she heard her mother's voice in the distance.

"Take care of yourself, sweetheart."

CHAPTER TWENTY –
The Battle of Mik-Mag

Umar and Adn marched their force from the camp site. The army moved slowly behind the two princes. Rain slicked across their golden attire and golden swords, their faces, their heads, and the horses they rode. Mud filled the path in front of them.

Prince Umar was eager to see what the elders of the City of Mik-Mag could offer for aid. There was no one else to help them this far away from the Golden Gates. The burnt lands, mud, and feeling of being forgotten made it seem as if there was no other hope for them.

Even without a battle to fight, despair was beginning to fill the hearts of his men. As they rode, they saw the after-math of other battles that had occurred here. Would their fate be the same?

A single road lead into the city of Mik-Mag. The army reached it, turned, and followed Prince Umar to the building where they first met Cassini. He stood outside on the steps, watching as children ran through the city, laughing as they played in the mud and rain.

"Cassini," said Prince Umar, smiling down from his horse.

"Young Princes, or Your Highness," said Cassini. His words were polite, but his voice held the edge of rudeness. "Your brother is here, begging the elders for aid, but why should we help you? You come down from your high castles and Golden Gates to ask for our help. We shouldn't..."

"Enough!" said an elder, as he walked out of the building.

"Why? Why should we aid these young kids?" Cassini asked. His voice was strong, confident.

The elder looked into Cassini's eyes. "We aren't going to aid them," he said.

Prince Kaf walked outside, muttering under his breath, "What bad timing. My brothers and the whole army are here to see my failure."

He tried to smile as he walked over to greet Umar. "I'm sorry, my brother. They would not listen to me."

"What did you say to them?" asked Umar.

"I asked if they would ride to the south with us, but the elder was worried. He said that no one comes back from the south. The elders said if we only knew what lives in the south, we would not go, either. They are worried for their own skin, but I don't blame them."

Umar's face grew grave. "This really puts a fork in our plans," he said. "We need more riders for this task. I'll talk to them. You go get a horse."

He trotted angrily toward Cassini and the elder, who were still arguing about something.

"Listen, Cassini, when I'm dead, then you can make decisions," the elder yelled. "Right now, I'm the elder."

"Yeah? Let's see how long that will last," Cassini said, and he walked away with his bodyguards.

Umar called after Cassini. "Is that how you talk to your elder?"

"Suck it," Cassini said rudely.

"Let him go," the elder said. "It's better if he leaves."

"Why is he here, if he has that kind of power?" Umar asked. "A lot of Norm people live here. Why haven't you rebuilt the city?"

"Cassini's father was an elder before me. It seems that young people always think they know best, but they hardly wait or listen. I know his father would have wanted a strong city. Cassini wants it, too, but we cannot build the city anymore. We do not have the drive to. In these lands, with this weather and no sun, why try?"

Umar tried to find a good response to this, but the elder was already speaking again.

"I'm guessing you're here to ask me why I said no to your request," he said. "Your brother came to us asking for aid, but nothing we can provide could help you down in the south. If you go, you'll never come back. No one ever does!"

"But we need you," Umar said, "And if we can defeat the darkness, it will benefit you, too."

"You really are the High King's son," the elder said. "You're both alike, always pushing, pushing, but never stopping to ask why. For that, I'll not let the few riders I have go to the south. If you really want to know why, you should ask your O-Father. If you knew what lives and grows there, you would never think about going there."

The elder sputtered, caught his breath, and looked back into Prince Umar's face, which seemed to harden like stone.

"I know my warning will not stop you," the elder said. "Go. Go and see for yourself, but heed my words. Do not bring that evil here! We have seen enough death."

The elder scanned Umar's face, but Umar stared back with his emotionless white eyes and a stern face. In a deep voice, he said, "We fear nothing but the Lord. I was tasked with a simple request, to push back any evil that could bring harm to the lands of Amer. This means if an evil is growing in the south, we'll ride to the south."

"See!" the elder cried. "See! You're just like your father. He thought this evil was easy to fight, too, but no army, no king, and no shah can fight back this evil. With this evil comes dark clouds and a darker curse."

"What curse?" asked Umar.

"Oh, yes, the curse," said the Elder. "With this curse comes..."

"Run!" a Norm called, as he ran past the army and the elder. "Run!"

"What's going on?" asked the elder as the man dashed past.

"Spiders!" the man gasped. "Asward!"

Behind him, the spiders were running into the city. Their long legs, sharp as a hundred knives, stabbed into the walls of the houses they climbed. As the civilians of Mik-Mag tried to run, the spiders grabbed them, ripping their flesh or biting them, while the Asward soldiers atop them stabbed with their spears and slashed with their swords.

Screams filled the air, and blood began to flow.

"Za-Alm! Line Up!" yelled Umar. Immediately, the soldiers took their positions, and the prince stood behind them.

The spiders ran straight toward them. There was no time to think, and barely time to act. The elder, white faced and wide-eyed, ran into the building as the battle for the city of Mik-Mag began.

The spiders and Aswards ripped the civilians of the city limb from limb. The spider's sharp legs made strange, airy noises as they crawled around on the city walls.

Even the spiders' hearts filled with jealousy and greed for the Northern Kin's golden attire. They became more aggressive, hissing and huffing as they lunged toward the army.

"Hold! Hold!" Umar shouted, as his men shifted nervously behind him. There was no time to think now.

As the spiders drew closer, Umar saw the Asward soldiers riding them. He noticed their swords and spears before he saw the bows. The Asward soldiers let loose a stream of arrows that pierced into Umar's army, killing some men in the front line.

The Golden Army was unprepared for this fight. The large spiders, larger than any they had ever seen before, were all that they could focus on.

"Fire," the Asward captain called, and another round of arrows flew into the Golden Army, hitting many soldiers in their face legs.

"Ah!" the cries of Golden Soldiers falling to the ground was unbearable. "Ah!"

The attack filled Umar's heart with rage. "Za-Jaa! Charge!" The soldiers of the Golden Army lunged forward, swinging their swords of gold with all their might as the line of spiders collided with them. Their blades found their marks, but the spider's legs were thick and rock-like. Some of the swords bent or broke.

"Aim for the riders," Adn called as he rode through the battle, taking out as many Asward soldiers as he could.

"Ah! Ah!" said Kaf, and he jumped off his horse onto the top of an asward soldier as he rode by on his spider. With one flick of his wrist, Kaf cut the rider's head from his body. Kaf and the lifeless Asward tumbled off the spider, but the spider kept on running.

"Get back here!" Kaf yelled, and he chased the spider through the battle.

Umar was covered by his soldiers. He watched, yelling orders to his brothers and the soldiers on the front line.

They were finally getting the fight they wanted, but it was overwhelming. His young fighters were not prepared to fight these ruthless, enormous spiders. The spiders climbed the broken houses and crept around the walls, dodging the Golden Soldiers, who attacked them without a plan.

"Za-Alm! Line Up!" yelled Umar, and Golden Soldiers ran back to form another line in front of Umar. Kaf and Adn galloped into the front line, shouting.

In the distance, the sound of a horn blared.

"Prince Umar, I see more soldiers coming!" Zuda's hands shook as he pointed toward Saint Lawrence and his soldiers, who were now arriving at the edge of the city. Shouts and screams of pain filled the air anew.

"So be it!" said Umar. He kept his face expressionless, but he pulled out his sword as his men prepared for another round of attacks. The Asward soldiers, who carried bone-like swords, fought in ways that Adu never taught them, and the spiders seemed desperate to get the shiny golden armor from his men.

"Charge!" yelled the captain of the dark-armored men, and the men and spiders ran forward toward the lines of the Golden Army.

"Za-Jaa! Charge!" yelled Umar, and all the soldiers ran forward to join the battle they never thought would come.

The rain continued to fall, and despair seeped into their skin as bodies and limbs filled the streets.

The two armies clashed. Spiders bit the Northern Kin while the riders on top aimed spears right at their heads. The Northern Kin were fighting for their lives. Many Golden Soldiers had already fallen, but the princes at least were skilled in their art.

Umar swung his sword left and right, slaying the dark-armored soldiers one by one. His face never changed, but inside, an anger he had never known before grew and took on a life of its own. He began killing without thought.

"Fight!" Adn called to his men. "Fight back these evil foes!" Both his swords were dark with blood. He cut spiders with so much power that their rock-like skin fell apart. "Die! Die!" he called, but without warning, a spider's leg pierced his horse. Adn swung high and stabbed the spider's eyes as he fell.

The spider screamed and fell back.

"You think I'm done?" said Adn as he pushed himself back onto his feet. He kept fighting beside other Golden Soldiers, slaying the saint's small army and as many of the spiders as he could get.

As he swung his sword at another spider's legs, Kaf shot his golden bow. He always hit his target—Asward soldiers, spider's eyes, and even into Ingie's horse.

"Ah! Ah! Ah!" yelled Kaf.

Behind him, the elder and civilians of the city emerged from their hiding places.

"Fire!" yelled the elder, and the civilians of Mik-Mag fired iron-tipped arrows into the dark-armored forces. "Fire!" he yelled again. Another round zinged through the air, piercing many through their armor. Some dark soldiers were killed, but more were wounded.

"Keep it going, boys," said Cassini as he emerged from his building and joined the battle.

Now all the soldiers of the Northern Kin and the civilians from the city of Mik-Mag stood side by side, fighting for what good was left in their world. They fought the evil that was growing not only in the battle, but in their hearts, as well.

"Kill them all!" yelled the soldiers of the north, and they began pushing back the Saint's army. With every move, more dark-armored soldiers fell. With the aid of the civilians, Ingie and Hassen realized they were overpowered.

"Fall back!" yelled Ingie, as his soldiers began scattering and fleeing. Their weapons fell from their hands as they ran away. A few soldiers fell behind, and they were caught by Umar's soldiers, who called, "Get them! Bring them back to the prince!"

Without their riders, the spiders began to flee, too. Even as they fled, their screeches and screams filled the hearts of the Northern Kin with fear. They understood that they hadn't won. They had only postponed their fate.

"Keep going!" Ingie shouted to his men. "Run!" Suddenly, he rounded on Hassen, who was galloping along beside him.

"You!" Ingie shouted. "You did this to us. You stay here!" He kicked high, knocking Hassen off his horse. As he rode off, he laughed. "I hope you die here."

"Don't leave me here!" cried Hassen, struggling to get to his feet and follow the dark army, hoping to avoid his fate with the people he had betrayed.

Behind him, Umar finally caught his breath and began to get his bloodlust under control.

"Go, and see if anyone is left," he called. "Bring them to me, so they might answer for their crimes." His eye twitched. He didn't even notice that his sword was mucky with blood and black pus from cutting through spider skin.

"Help! Please help!" yelled a few Golden Soldiers, who lay wounded throughout the city. Citizens began coming to them, helping them off the streets into the broken buildings and make-shift shelters.

"Did you see those spiders?" asked a Golden Soldier named Zada, as the young boys finally started to look around them. Now that the action was subsiding, they could take in the blood, the body parts filling the streets, and the screams of injured women and children from around the city.

Many of their kin were dead, including the youngest. He lay on his side, eyes open and glassy, with a spider leg pierced through his chest.

"Prince! They killed Azui!!" cried Zada. He ran to Azui's body, pulled out the spider leg, and scooped the dead boy into his arms. "Someone, help! Please!" tears ran down his cheeks as he carried the little body, still dripping with blood, to Prince Umar. All the soldiers stopped, looking at their friend as he stumbled through the ruins with Azui.

Their family member died. This was something they never thought would happen. They reached out their hands, touching Azui's body as Zada carried him through their midst. Only a few hours ago, they were joking with him in the camp while the rain drenched them, but now blood filled the city, and the rain still fell.

"Oh!" cried Umar, when he finally saw Azui's body through the crowd of battered men.

The site shattered Umar's resolve. His face crumpled, and he started to cry.

"Put him down. Put his body down."

Umar's voice broke as he looked on the dead body of the youngest kin of his family. His blood was on Umar's hands.

"I never wanted this!" yelled Umar. He pulled back his head and shouted obscenities at the ever-dark sky. As the Golden Soldiers watched their prince break down, darkness filled their hearts

CHAPTER TWENTY-ONE – Castle of Blayney, Part 1

Nimra and Ismail walked slowly through the overgrown forest. The long roots of the tree filled their path, and the sun's rays were blocked by the branches of half-dead trees. The only light came from the torch Nimra carried.

"Why did we leave her there?" Nimra asked. "We can go back and help. Maybe she fell and banged her head, and that's why she forgot who she was."

"I'm sorry, Nimra, but she does not seem right in the mind," Ismail said. "Her memories are fading, but not all forgotten. I just don't think we can help her. She seemed hostile, and we can't travel to the West-lands kingdom with her fighting us the whole way. We need to focus on getting out of these woods. If a little spider can trick and trap us, just imagine what else is out here. Let's push on. We need to find Laenatan."

As Nimra wiped a stray tear from her cheek, Ismail hacked at the long roots sticking out of the ground. Anger boiled inside him, and like the dark woods, it spread evil.

"Slow down," Nimra said. "Why are we rushing? Are you sure we're heading the right way?"

"Your Grandmother said we need to reach the Castle of Blayney," he said. "If only we had Laenatan, he could fly ahead and let us know where the castle might be, but yet, we're still stuck in these woods!" yelled Ismail.

"Stop rushing ahead!" Nimra said. "Do you want that spider, or something even worse, to find us?" She reached over to Ismail, touching his arm with her hand to calm him down as she searched his white eyes. "What are you freaking out about?"

"I'm sorry," said Ismail, and he lowered his swords. "These woods are not like the High King's Forest. I'm having a hard time focusing. It's like there's something messing with my head. Do you feel it? It's like something or someone is knocking, trying to get in."

"No, I feel fine," Nimra said. "I don't hear a knock, but do not worry. I'll take the lead, while you just calm down. I really don't want to see that creepy spider again just because you feel light-headed and angry."

She tried to joke, and it lightened the mood for a moment, but as she walked ahead, it seemed that the thick forest had no end to it. They walked for hours with barely any sunrays to help. It was difficult to tell if it was day or night. While light couldn't make it past the trees, the drizzling rain did.

Finally, Nimra stop, shook her soaked hair away from her face, and said. "What now? It seems like we have been walking in circles for hours, and this rain is not helping us."

"Yeah. I don't know. It's hard to find a high point here because the trees are huge. Maybe we should try to climb one and see what's around." Ismail smiled, happy to finally have a clear thought that was actually a good idea.

"Okay," said Nimra. "I'll climb up and see where to go. You can hold onto the torch, but do not burn anything. These woods are so dry, they could burn in spite of the rain."

Nimra's Qazam skills kicked in the moment she grabbed the tree, and she moved up the trunk with ease and speed.

"Whoah!" Ismail yelled as he watched her climb. "You good at this!"

"Be quiet, you idiot," Nimra retorted, but the fun had returned to their conversation, and for a few minutes, they both felt better. Then Nimra disappeared behind the dark branches, and Ismail was left alone again.

These woods were so dismal compared to the High King's Forest. Where he grew up, there were animals, birds, and flowers of every kind, but here, it appeared that all the animals had died or left. Ismail strolled around the tree, holding the torch high, when a quiet movement caught his eye.

There. In the forest ahead of him, a shadow slowly meandered through the trees, without pattern or purpose.

Ismail took a step forward, and then a few more steps, quietly getting closer to the figure.

Like Nimra's mother, this appeared to be a person. Someone else was lost in these woods. Ismail heard the figure talking to himself as he drew near.

Ismail hid behind a tree and watched. He remembered Igor's tricks, and he was reluctant to put himself and Nimra in danger again. Still, this appeared to be a man, one who was very confused. He wore full metal armor made from fine iron, and at his hip he wore a massive sword the size of Nimra and Ismail together.

"What his deal? Why is he here, and who in his right mind want come to these woods?" Ismail thought to himself. He moved closer through the browning brush around the tree and caught the echo of familiar words.

"Why? Why am I here? What am I doing?"

Ismail looked beyond the man, hoping to see a house or a castle or even a horse, but there were only dark tree trunks, wet with rain.

"Why? Why?" the man said, stumbling through the dark. Ismail pulled back behind the tree trunk completely.

"This is interesting," Ismail said to himself. "He's repeating the same words that Nimra's mother used, but why?"

The man stumbled again. Ismail hid the torchlight the best he could and tried to sneak away without attracting his notice.

Then Nimra yelled. "Ismail! Ismail!"

Ismail jumped. "She was the one who said not to yell!" he whispered to himself, and he started to move again toward the tree she had climbed.

The stranger. Ismail whirled around to see the armored man standing straight up, alert, looking upward at the tree Nimra sat in. Ismail felt a prickle of danger. What would happen to Nimra if the stranger got to her before he did?

Ismail rushed forward with his torch, but he spoke calmly to the strange man.

"Good Sayid," he said, "Can you help me?"

"I'm no saint," the man said, and then his eyes opened wider. "Oh, you're a young boy. What are you doing here in these dark and forgotten woods?"

"We—" Ismail started, and then changed his wording to keep Nimra safe. "I got lost."

"Lost? This place is no place for a young boy. Where are you from?"

"I'm from Castle of Blayney," Ismail said. "My family and I got split up near the woods, and I've been trying to find my way out, but this place is confusing and I don't know where to go."

Ismail tried to look as innocent as he could as he moved closer to the armored man. "May I ask who you are, and what are you doing here?"

"I...I can't remember who I am, but just like you, I got lost in these woods," the man said. "I'm also looking for a way out of this thick forest, but these trees are so big that they block any sun that might reach below." He stared into Ismail's face, and Ismail began to feel uncomfortable. He was just about to say something when the man spoke again.

"What's odd to me the idea that you're from the Castle of Blayney," the man said. "No families live there now. No one in their right mind would want to visit that place, not since the dark clouds spread into that land. Something odd happened there. Rumors are that the people who lived there lost their minds."

Ismail jumped at the new information. "Yes, that's why we left," he said. "We hoped to find safety. But where are you from, if not the castle?"

"The last thing I can remember was being sent from the King to a city, but my fellow knights and I got lost once we got close to these lands. I always wonder where they ended up. I wonder, are my fellow brothers alright? But I can't remember what city I was tasked to visit. I can't even remember the names of my fellow knights. The only thing I remember is that people were looking for a child, fighting over a boy."

Ismail glanced at the knight again, briefly taking in his armor and sword. Once, his father had spoken of the great knights from the West-lands, who had been sent to aid him during the Golden Age. King Alm always said they were the best knights he had ever seen.

"You're a knight? What king do you serve?" Ismail asked.

"Yes, I'm a knight of Hazens, the old king of the West-lands, but that's all I know. I don't know if I was a good knight, or how long I have been a knight. However, once a knight, always a knight, and the knights of the West-lands fight for the old king. He tasked us with protecting the West-lands, but these times are hard on us. We've been sent to far lands to fight, to battle an enemy that cannot be seen. Most of us become lost or confused, and we lose ourselves." As he spoke, the knight's face became sad, almost vacant, and his voice trailed away weakly at the end.

"My O-Father told me great things about the knights from the West-lands," Ismail said. "He always spoke about the heavy armor they wore and the great-swords they carried into battle. Great knight, may I ask you to aid us—I mean me—to find a way out of these woods and get to the Castle of Blayney?"

"Your father spoke the truth," the knight said. "We hold ourselves to high standards. And yes, it would be my honor to aid you in this quest. It will give me something to focus on, and perhaps I will begin to think clearly again." He sighed and rubbed his face with one hand. "I've already forgotten your name," he said.

"Thank you, kind knight of Hazens! I'm Ismail."

"I remember my name!" cried the knight, and he knelt on the ground, plunging his great-sword into the earth in front of him. He held it with both hands as he said, "I'm Aikiba, knight of King Hasen. I promise to help you to get back to your family, but please promise me one thing in return."

"Of course, Aikiba," said Ismail.

"Please. Please help me find out more about who I was before I got lost in these woods," said Aikiba, and he stood again and sheathed his great-sword.

"I promise, I'll aid you in your quest," Ismail said. He beckoned to Aikiba. "Come. I want you to meet someone."

He led Aikiba back through the woods to Nimra, who was pacing in front of the tree she had climbed and calling for Ismail.

"Ismail! Where are you!"

"I'm here," he yelled, and he waved at her as she turned to face him.

"Oh, I am so glad to see you. Where did you run off to?" Nimra appeared slightly angry, and then she looked scared when she saw the massive shadow of the knight moving forward through the trees.

"Behind you!" she shouted, and she pulled out her bow, nocked an arrow and shot to the right of Ismail's head.

"No!" yelled Ismail as the arrow whizzed past his ear. It hit Aikiba's armor and bounced off.

"Ouch!" Aikiba said. "Put that down, silly girl. Wait—your ears. I have never seen ears like that before. Who are you?"

Nimra, who was already reaching for another arrow, shouted at Aikiba.

"Who am I? It's none of your business. Ismail, did he attack you? Who is he, and why is he here?"

"Relax, Nimra," Ismail said. He walked over to her and lowered her bow. "He's a knight from West-lands. My O-Father spoke about the great knights from those lands and their king. Come, put your bow away. He's promised to help us."

"Nimra stood tensely for a moment, and then she shouldered her bow. Her voice still sounded angry when she spoke. "I guess you want to know what I saw when I was up in that tree, right? But I was only up there for a few minutes, and you already found another person. How do you know if we can trust him?"

She didn't even try to be polite in front of Aikiba, but he seemed more surprised than offended.

"Who are you?" Aikiba asked. "And why are you here? I begin to feel that the story Ismail told me was a lie."

"Listen, Nimra," Ismail said. "You went up the tree, and I heard Aikiba talking to himself. I felt out the situation and discovered that he's a friend, an honorable knight from the West-lands."

"This is interesting," Aikiba said, glancing between Nimra and Ismail. "A young girl with pointed ears, and a young boy with a light glow to him. If my guess is correct, you're both from beyond the Golden Gates—but how did the two of you get here?"

"Well, you're correct, we are from the North," said Ismail. He reached into his bag, pulled out the rusted crown and placed it onto his head. Aikiba looked at Ismail for a second, and then his mouth fell open in surprise.

"Oath-keeper!" said Aikiba. He fell to his knees and said. "How the fates are cruel to us! We should have known!"

"You know the oath?" Nimra asked. "How could the fates be cruel to you?"

"Yes, all people from the West-lands know the oath," the knight said. "They know that someday there will come a boy who will draw back the darkness that spreads through the lands of Amer.

Aikiba's voice grew quieter, and his words seemed etched with pain. "We did not know the oath-keeper would come from the north, though. Now all of our young boys are dead, or in hiding. The ones that are left are hunted by the Oligarchs, who are charged with stopping the oath-keeper from taking on the quest to stop Ibies, but here you are. You are hope in the darkest of places."

"There's still so much I do not know," Ismail said. "Who are the Oligarchs? Who is Ibies?"

"I can't say much about these subjects, but the Oligarchs are the corrupted Norms from the Middle-lands who are tempted by power, by Ibies. They spread only evil and bring death from the sky. Now a curse spreads like fire in the hearts of men, and it's doing a number on me." Aikiba tried to laugh as he made fun of his own forgetfulness, but the joke didn't bring any smiles.

"The candle-maiden named Marta spoke about this curse," Ismail said. "We need to stay clear of this darkness, but the maidens never spoke about the Oligarchs. They only said we need to head to Castle of Blayney."

"I told you, Oath-keeper, that place is destroyed," said Aikiba. "All the people have died."

"I know, Aikiba, but we need to visit the castle and see a scholar there," Ismail said. "We need his aid to get a sword from the Dragon Mountains. We might not stay long, but we do have to ask our questions."

"I really do not know what you speak of," Aikiba said. "Dragons? A scholar? I don't know about these things, but I'll fulfill my promise to aid you."

"Good!" Nimra said, and she nodded her head firmly. "Let's go. I saw the edge of the forest when I was up in the tree, and there's a road that will lead us to the west. Once we get to it, we might see Laenatan."

"Laenatan?" Aikiba said. "Who is Laenatan?"

"He's the large owl that travels with us," Nimra said. Aikiba blinked, as if he had questions to ask, but Ismail was already speaking.

"Sounds like a plan," Ismail said. "Here's the torch. You can lead."

Nimra's words brought back their cheer, and they walked hope in their footsteps.

"I can't believe you shot me," said Aikiba as they made their way through the trees.

"Oh, don't be a baby," Nimra said.

Aikiba laughed for real this time, and the sound echoed in his helmet.

CHAPTER TWENTY-TWO – Blood and Death

The Qazam royal family walked with their few guards into the Castle of the High King, which had been built into the face of the mountain. They headed toward the Tower of Light.

With ever step they took, the Northern Kin stared. None of them had ever seen a Qazam in the castle before.

There were a lot of kin in the castle to stare at the Qazams, too. The castle served as a single home that housed all the kin of the High King. There were more than a million bricks. The ceilings of each hallway and room were built with fine white stones. Gold and green gems were crafted into the walls, but none of these treasures stopped the Qazam royal party. They looked only ahead as they marched to the Tower of Light.

Their intent was clear, even though they didn't say a word to the Northern Kin watching them. People stepped to the side to allow them to pass. At first, the hearts of the royal party were heavy, and speaking with the High King was all they thought about. As they reached the tower, the beautiful snow that always fell but never reached the ground and the glow of light from the tower eased their pain and worries a little.

For a few moments, they understood the power of this light. It brought hope and peace, but their duty was clear. They didn't pause to take in the beauty or the fact that the top of the tower was open, allowing the light to spread across the northern lands as far as the Golden Gates.

As the Qazam royal family made it to the tower step, the loud voice of a captain sounded in the corridor.

"Halt! None who are not worthy shall step into the tower of light."

Anger filled Idun's face. "We are not worthy in your eyes?"

"I said no one shall pass unless they are worthy," the captain said. "If you try to pass, I shall take you into my custody, Qazam."

The Qazam guards moved closer to the Royal family, but they drew their swords reluctantly, hoping to avoid a fight with the notable Golden Guard of the High King.

"Let us not fight amongst ourselves," said Meltôriel, and her voice calmed the men around her. "Come now, put away your swords. No blood should be drawn today."

"My Lady Meltôriel, I apologize," said the captain, and he sheathed his sword. "You are worthy to enter, my Lady."

As the Qazam guards stood down, Idun whispered to Meltôriel. "Go, and speak to him. You know what to say, my love."

Meltôriel nodded and walked up the white marble stairs alone. With every step, the light around her grew. As she entered the tower, all the anger in her heart cleared and her worries dissipated. In spite of her mission, she felt only ease and peace.

High King Alm sat upon his throne. Amir lay near him, and Zubair stood at the bottom of the throne, watching as Meltôriel approached.

"I know why you came, but please, do not stop me from hearing your words, my Lady Meltôriel," said the High King. "Why are you here, and why is Idun outside with his guards?"

"High King, we come in peace and only want some of your time alone," said Meltôriel.

"Why?" Zubair asked, drawing his sword. "None of the Qazam have ever come here, and honestly, we do not trust any of you close to our King. Golden Guard, come and take Meltôriel and her friends to the dungeons below!"

"Enough, Zubair!" King Alm commanded. "I want to hear what Meltôriel and her husband have to say. Zubair, please go, and take the Golden Guards with you."

"Of course, my King." Zubair gave Meltôriel a cold stare as he walked away.

"Send Idun to me," King Alm called to Zubair. Zubair bowed and left the throne room, and Alm rose from his throne. As he walked down the steps, Amir watched him.

"High King, I want to say thank you for talking to us in person," Meltôriel said. "This kingdom is something I have never seen before, and the snow is so beautiful."

Alm stopped in front of Meltôriel, towering over her. His long gray hair hung straight around his face, giving him a severe look.

"Thank you for your kind words, Meltôriel, but may we speak about why you are here?" he said.

"You know why we are here!" said Idun, pacing angrily into the throne room. "You treat me like a dog, calling me in whenever you want."

"Enough!" Amir's deep voice rumbled through the room as he stood and pawed his way down the steps to stand beside the High King. Everyone went silent until King Alm spoke again.

"I know why you are here, Meltôriel and Idun. By now you know the vision I saw. You can and should blame me for any harm that might come upon you son. You know a darkness is growing in the Middle-lands, and last time we tried to defeat it, we lost our friends, our families, and our kin. Now I feel something worse is coming, but my visions are fading. I hardly even see the princes now, and even Amir's visions are blocked by the Cursed One."

"Is there no hope?" Meltôriel whispered.

"Yes, we have hope," Amir rumbled. "We hope in the form of a small boy who needs our aid now, so we can't afford to fight amongst ourselves."

"I haven't heard you speak since the Golden Age, Amir," said Idun, "But if you're right, then who is this boy?"

"He is my son," King Alm said. "His name is Ismail. He left with a young Qazam girl named Nimra."

Shock filled Idun's voice.

"What? You let your youngest son pass the Golden Gates?"

"Nimra," said Meltôriel. "I knew her mother and her grand-mother. They were both candle-maidens, but how does your son fit into all of this, King Alm?"

The High King spoke slowly, gravely. "There's an Arch Dragon in the far mountains of the West-lands. This Arch Dragon possesses a sword that can kill the Cursed One. The candle-maidens tasked Ismail and Nimra to get the sword."

Amir's deep voice filled the empty space between the High King and the Qazam royals. "Ismail needs our help, if he has any hope of reaching that place in the West-lands, but dark tales are being told of those lands now. The dark clouds and the curse have been spread there, and the king of the West-lands has gone crazy."

"He's right," King Alm said. "We need to send my son aid, and we'll send more riders to help your son, as well. Will you agree to stand with me in this dark time, even though we are fighting blind?"

"We want our son and the other Qazam youth to be safe," Idun said. "They are too young, and they have never been to the south. However, I agree we need to send more riders to the Middle-lands. I cannot lose my son!"

"You will not lose him, my old friend. Meltôriel, I promise you, as well, that you will see your son once again. Now come with me, and I'll inform you of our plans."

"Shall I ride south, too?" Idun asked.

"No. We will keep our three rules that we made when the Golden Gates were built, and never transgress against them," said Alm.

Idun looked worried, but he was distracted as Amir turned, nodded at the High King, and walked away.

"Where is he going?" Idun asked.

"Do not worry," the High King said. "He'll be back. We all have our duty to this kingdom."

He led them out of the throne room and toward his personal chamber to discuss his plans. The light from the windows slowly dimmed behind them.

CHAPTER TWENTY-THREE – Reality

The Golden Soldiers stood in the mud. Blood and dirt from the battle covered their golden attire, and despair filled their hearts as they buried their dead kin. Tears ran down every face.

Even the princes walked with dejection as they visited the graves of their kin. The black clouds still twisted above their heads, the rain never stopped, everything was wet, and none of them knew what to do. Meanwhile, the dark-armored soldiers holed up confidently in their retreat, confident that no one dared to touch them.

Throughout the city, spider bodies and legs lay scattered, hanging from the roofs, trees, and walls. The spider's purple blood mixed with rain and flooded in the streets as their bodies began to rot, but none of the civilians seemed fazed by this. In fact, they seemed shocked at how the first battle had shattered the Golden Army.

"You know this is only the beginning," the civilians said.

Cassini shouted his anger at the elders. "That was only a few of the Asward soldiers. Saint Lawrence from the Tower of Muslakh will follow with more of them, and you know what happens in that tower!"

"You think we do not all know this?" the elder said. "You act as if this attack was the first, or the last. Should we cower every time they ride here? Should we let them take our children and turn them against us, or kill them?"

As the civilians looked at the dead bodies of the dark-armored soldiers that lay moldering throughout the city, the elder tried to reason with them.

"We should aid the princes," he said. "We should fight back this evil, not for us, but for our kin! If we stay here and just let them come into our city, we'll all be dead, or worse! We could be taken to Muslakh and our fates would be sealed."

Cassini shouted angrily at the elder, demanding the attention of the civilian crowd. "You speak like you know! Do you think we stand a chance against Saint Lawrence, with his black spiders and Asward riders? No! We must stand down. We cannot afford to help the princes, and you must be off your rocker to think you can place hope in them."

"Your arrogance will be your downfall," the elder said quietly.

"Your failures are your own, old man," said Cassini. He stalked away with his body guards as the other civilians looked at each other, confused and afraid.

"Who else agrees with him?" the elder asked. "If you do, join him. Walk away right now, because those princes are our only hope of getting rid of Saint Lawrence now."

A few of the civilians meandered after Cassini, but many stayed.

"Good," the elder said, as the remaining citizens bunched around him. "Since we are all in agreement, let's go speak with the princes."

They moved as one past the dead bodies and spider's legs, through the mud and the rain to where the princes camped outside the city, near the graves of their dead. With the elder's invitation, a few of them moved forward to greet the princes, who stood over the graves. Prince Umar was giving a speech.

"I promised this would not happen," Umar said. "Now we fight to make sure our dead kin did not die in vain. I promised our brother, Azui, that I would protect him. I failed. I hope he will forgive me, and we hope all our fallen brothers are at peace. Meanwhile, for as long as we are in this dark place, we must bear our pain and carry on. We will fulfill the task that we were given!"

In the dim light, it was too difficult to see whether the wetness on Umar's cheeks were tears or raindrops. The elder and his men waited until Umar finished speaking, and then they approached the dismal, battered Golden Soldiers.

The elder cleared his throat. "Prince's and Northern Kin, we are sorry for your losses," he said.

"As we are for yours, elder," Umar said. "Thank you for coming to our aid. We would not have lived if you hadn't stepped in when you did."

"That's why we are here," the elder said. "We fear that this was not the last attack from Asward soldiers. Saint Lawrence will be close by if those spiders are this near to our city."

Kaf, who was glaring at the mud covering his boots, looked up sharply. "Who is the Saint?"

"The Saint is a cunning man," the elder said. "He came to us promising us coins and giving us fine gifts, but that snake's head is part of a bigger body. If the Asward soldiers are here, this only means Saint Lawrence is not far behind. We need to work together."

Adn tapped Umar on the shoulder. "May we talk to you for a minute?" he asked, and the elder politely excused the three princes. They moved toward the city's broken walls, whispering to each other.

"Do you believe the elder's information about a saint?" Adn asked. "Why would a religious Norm attack a city? It seems odd to me."

"Yes, but they talk as if they've battled these forces before," Umar said. "We need their help, and at least we can help them in return.

"It's your choice, brother," said Kaf. "We'll follow where you lead."

Within just a few minutes, the princes returned to the elder and his men.

"We will help you," Prince Umar said, "But we need to be fully honest with one other. Did the dark soldiers attack us because you told the Saint our whereabouts?"

The elder rubbed his chin thoughtfully. "Do you think there might be a spy among us?"

"How else would the Saint know we were here?" Umar asked. "Or do dark soldiers attack every day?"

"The princes are right," a civilian man said. "We could have a spy here!"

Conversation began buzzing among the civilians. The elder looked shocked and unhappy.

"Come into our tent and talk with us," Umar told him, clapping him on the shoulder. "If you want to aid us, then let's make our plans together."

The elder agreed, and he followed the princes into the tent while the civilians speculated whether or not there was really a spy—and if so, who would be foolish enough to try to make their own deal with Saint Lawrence?

CHAPTER TWENTY-FOUR – Castle of Blayney, Part 2

Ismail, Nimra and Aikiba emerged from the dark woods into a burnt, lightless land. The few plants that remained were withered. In spite of the constant rain, they were brown and dry, and they cracked or snapped when the legs of the travelers brushed them.

"This doesn't feel any better," Nimra said. "Are we making any progress on this task? Maybe we're not going the right way."

"We're headed west," Aikiba said. "That's where the castle should be. My memory isn't like it once was but I do feel like this is the way. I remember this rain."

"Let's at least move further away from these woods," Ismail said. He peered into the sky, hoping to spot Laenatan, but the clouds were too thick and dark to see much.

"I can't see Laenatan," he said. "How do rain and clouds like this happen here? Why is the land burnt?"

"It's been like this ever since the Vicar came from the south," Aikiba said. "He brought evil and spread chaos throughout the lands. Many people were killed, or worse, used as bait."

Ismail and Nimra stopped to listen, and shock filled their faces. "Wait," Ismail said. "Who is the Vicar?"

"I do not know much, but if I remember correctly, he's one of the Oligarchs we the knights of West-lands fought," Aikiba said. "We have no power to ride against him, but we tried. I rode with a few of my best knights against the Vicar. Most of my friends were slaughtered like pigs. I alone escaped."

"We need to stay clear of this Vicar and just get to the castle" said Nimra. Her face and her voice were both tight with worry. "We don't want to end up getting slaughtered like pigs either." They trudged forward through mud and ashes, and her voice grew quiet again. "I'm sorry to hear about your fellow knights," she told Aikiba. "May they rest in peace."

Aikiba nodded, and he swallowed hard.

"I'm sorry you can't find your friend, Laenatan," he said.

Silence fell between them again, and Ismail nudged them both forward.

"Let's keep moving and try not to get any attention," Ismail said.

Aikiba took the lead. His heavy gray armor clunked through the dead grass, and his enormous sword sometimes scratched at the ashy surface or broke the tops from dead bushes. Unlike Ismail and Nimra, though, his helmet covered his head and most of his face. Only his eyes showed, blinking back the rain, tears, and terror.

Nimra spoke quietly to Ismail as they followed Aikiba across the desolate plain.

"This Vicar that Aikiba mentioned," she said. "Do you think he might be at the castle? Something seems off to me. I feel like the scholar won't be any help to us."

"I know what you mean," Ismail said. "Something is off. I feel it, but I know we need to stick to our plans as much as we can. We need to head to the castle and find a way to reach the Dragon King. Aikiba said he doesn't remember the way to the West Kingdom. I feel so bad he got lost in those woods, like us. He must have been intelligent and strong, once."

Aikiba stopped in front of them, and he yelled. "Look!" He pointed toward the air as an enormous owl swooped down from the dark clouds.

"It's Laenatan!" Ismail's heart leapt, and he allowed the small burst of joy to fill his chest. Laenatan landed quietly, although his claws slipped a little in the muddy ashes. As soon as his wings were folded at his sides, the owl asked about their journey. His voice was weary and worried.

"Where were you?" Laenatan asked. "You took so long."

"We got lost," Ismail said. "The woods were dark, and no light was able to reach the ground through the thick branches. We ran into a spider in there..." Ismail shuddered, and Aikiba leaned close to Nimra and whispered.

"Why is he talking to a bird?"

I don't know how he's doing it," Nimra said. "He knew how to communicate with him since before we met."

"A spider," Laenatan said suddenly to Ismail. "You said you spoke to a spider? Why would you do such a thing? They aided Ibies in the fight against your father, during the battle of the far east lands!" Laenatan hopped closer to Ismail, snapping his beak at him.

"Never trust a spider again, Ismail."

"I won't," Ismail said. "After that experience, I don't think I can."

Laenatan bobbed his head up and down. "We have something else to focus on now," the owl said. "I flew to the castle. It's been destroyed, and all the young boys from the West-lands are hung around it."

"What?" Ismail gasped. "Did you see any soldiers?"

This got both Nimra's and Aikiba's attention.

"What about soldiers?" Nimra asked.

"Laenatan said he flew to the castle. It's been destroyed, and there are young boys hanging from the outer walls. "Why would someone hang young boys who can't defend themselves? We need to go help anyone who might still be alive there."

"Did you hear what you just said?" Nimra asked, and frustration edged her voice. "If there are dead bodies and the castle has been destroyed, why would we risk going there?"

Aikiba looked away, apparently trying to mind his own business, while Ismail and Nimra argued.

"Nimra I know you're worried," Ismail said. "I know that what we just experienced would scare anyone, but we need to push forward to the castle and help the Norms who need it. Or are we really willing to leave those who are in danger to die, just because we feel a little bit afraid?"

He moved closer to Nimra, and he gave her shoulders a comforting squeeze. She bit her lip.

"You're right," she said finally, "But if we see any signs of the Vicar, we're leaving. Promise me that."

"I promise," Ismail said, but even then, he realized he didn't know what lay ahead of them. So far, none of their circumstances could have been foreseen.

Ismail turned back to Laenatan. "It's helpful to know what we're heading toward," he said. "Thank you, Laenatan."

The giant owl bobbed his head. "I can fly beyond the Castle of Blayney and keep scouting for you," he said. "This seems to be the only way I can truly help."

"Yes, Laenatan," Ismail said. "I'm grateful for what you can do. Please find out what you can about the land west of the Castle. We will meet you there."

They walked in silence toward the Castle of Blayney, while Laenatan circled above them and then disappeared into the clouds.

Even in the darkness, they saw smoke in the distance, and the stink of burned flesh filled the air. Someone screamed, begging for death.

"I'm so uneasy," Nimra whispered, and Ismail nodded. Their faces were white and pinched.

As they moved forward, rainwater rushed in to fill their footprints. It appeared that the entire lower part of the castle was flooded. Most of the outer wall had crumbled. Bricks and broken stones scarred the inner courtyard around the castle. As Laenatan had said, dead boys hung from what was left of the walls.

If that wasn't enough to worry the group, the castle itself was lined with jail cells. The heavy steel cages were anchored along the outside of the castle, and they were filled with women—the mothers of the slaughtered boys.

"The Vicar must have made those cages," Aikiba whispered. "I think I remember now. He made them to torment those who once inhabited this place."

Ismail, Nimra and Aikiba entered the castle on the left side through a large hole.

"Do you hear that noise?" Aikiba asked. Faint cries rang through the dark castle, echoing against the broken stone.

"Yes," Ismail said. "It sounds like someone is crying. Let's look around. We need to find the source of the sound."

The companions trod carefully through the broken bricks and stones. When he spoke, Aikiba's voice sounded brittle. "This place is just a shell of the great castle it used to be," he said.

As they roamed the dark corridors, they came across a small room that contained a cage, like the ones outside. The rainwater dripped through a hole in the roof, flooding the floor of the cage, where a pitiful figure huddled.

"Hello," Ismail whispered gently, as they reached the cage. He knelt down, peering at the crying woman inside.

"Please, do not hurt me," the woman said. "I can't bear it any longer. Have mercy."

"We're not here to hurt you," said Ismail. "We came to help."

The woman raised her head.

"You're not part of the Vicar's forces?"

"No. We come from the North. My name is Ismail. This is Nimra, and this is Aikiba." He pointed at them in turn, and then turned back to the shivering woman.

"You're so young," she said. "Like my son was. Why are you so far from the protection of your Golden Gates?"

Ismail pulled his rusted crown from his pack and placed it on his head. The woman gaped, and then covered her mouth and sobbed, rocking back and forth against the wall where her cage was mounted.

"Oh, you—the oath-keeper—you came from the north!" she cried. "Our children lay dead from the hands of the Vicar. He was seeking the oath-keeper among our children here. His forces came with ciphers, hounds and demon dogs, but in the end, they were looking for you. We should have known. This is the true curse."

The woman doubled over in grief, burying her face against her knees.

"What do you mean?" Nimra asked. "Why would they attack you and your fellow kin, when they don't even know who the oath-keeper is?"

"We—the Norms—we have been looking for the oath-keeper for decades now," the woman said. "We heard that a boy would come and fight back against this darkness. Because of this, our children have been hunted by Ibies and his corrupted Oligarchs for years. They will do anything to kill the boy who might be the oath-keeper. To this end, Ibies allows his Oligarchs to terrorize anyone who might have information on the boy."

The woman lifted her head and stared at Ismail. "Ibies was looking in the wrong place," she said. "If he had known where you were, then maybe our children would have been safer during the past hundred years. Now the torment has finally reached our home, this castle."

She blinked, and sat up a little straighter. Her voice took on a sudden strength. "You must go," she said. "You must leave this place. This is not a place where the oath-keeper should roam."

"Ismail nodded, and he reached for the gated door of her cage. "We must all get out of here," he said.

"No, this is my fate now," the woman said, and she pulled his hands away from the door. "There are more than twenty cages here filled with mothers like me. We have all lost our sons, so living now has no meaning for us. Like the others, I must die here, as close to my son as I can be."

"Please come with us," Ismail said, and he reached for the door of her cage again. "Do you really think this is what your son would have wanted?"

"I would be no help to you," she said. "My fate is sealed, and the curse takes its toll on me. If you are the oath-keeper, then I beg one thing of you. Stop this cycle of death, and free my people from these shackles."

With great effort, the woman peeled Ismail's hands away from the steel bars once again. Her voice was raspy from crying, but her face held both resignation and hope. "I am Mehreen from the Castle of Blayney," she said. "This is the place where my family and I must lie."

Ismail's hands moved toward the cage a third time, but Aikiba's armored glove rested on Ismail's shoulder and pulled him away.

"She made her choice, Ismail," Aikiba said. "We must keep moving."

Ismail nodded, but tears flowed down his cheeks.

"You will not be forgotten, Mehreen," he said. "I will fulfill my oath, lest this curse swallow us whole, as it has so many others."

He turned quickly away, trying to hide his pain. Behind him, Mehreen's faint voice whispered. "Thank you. Thank you, oath-keeper."

The group made their way into the large castle chamber. The silence here was heavy and ominous. It was dark in the corridors, although screams and cries still echoed through them. A few candles provided small clouds of yellow light.

"We need to help Mehreen, and anyone who still lives in this castle, lest this be our fate, too," said Ismail.

"Who do you think left these candles here?" said Nimra.

As they moved deeper into the building, they found light red carpet, fine paintings, and white stone swords hanging as decorations against the walls.

"This place must have been incredibly wealthy once," she whispered.

"I do not know, but I feel we must be on guard," Aikiba said. He drew his great-sword.

"Over here!" Ismail whispered. "I think I've found the inner chamber."

"I don't think this is a good idea," said Nimra, but Ismail led the company through an odd-shaped doorway. A dark shadow rose in the corner, near a window that looked out over the back of the ruined courtyard.

"You there, boy!" the shadow hissed at Ismail. "Are you wearing a crown?"

"Who are you?" Aikiba's voice thundered, and he stepped forward, defending Ismail and Nimra with his own body.

"Oh, you are a knight of the West-lands," the shadow said. "How far have you traveled? I'm Sultan, the scholar of this castle." The shadow shuffled forward, laughing unpleasantly as he looked at each of the travelers in turn. His eyes rested on Ismail's face. "It appears that you are the oath-keeper."

Ismail spoke as bravely as he could. "Sultan the scholar, we are sent from the candle-maidens.

"Oh, I know, I know, but you still have not answered my question." Sultan's voice held anger or impatience. "Just say what I need to hear." He laughed again. Something about the sound reminded Ismail of the spider in the forest.

"Are you well, or are you sick and demented?" Ismail asked. "This place is completely destroyed. The children are dead, and the mothers are dying in cages. Why?"

"You ask a lot of questions, but secrets of this place must remain untold," Sultan said. "Are you really the oath-keeper, or just another pawn of fate? Come, sit down, and let's talk."

"No," Ismail said. "There's something wrong. I feel a darkness coming."

Aikiba nodded, still pointing his great-sword at Sultan's face. "We have no time for pleasantries," he said.

"Oh, oh," Sultan said, clapping his hands and laughing again. He pushed forward into the light, so that the group could see his gaunt face and long, white beard. "You really must be the oath-keeper. Friends like this are hard to come by these days."

His laughter broke off suddenly, and his voice became bitter. "I remember once when this castle was a great haven for Norms fleeing the Middle-lands and those fleeing from the mad king of the West-lands," Sultan said. "We were used. We never received any help from the High King or King Hazens. Finally, someone came and gave me power for a small...trade. You see, Oath-keeper, I waited for you, but who can stop this darkness now?"

"You serpent scum!" said Aikiba, and he swung his great-sword at Sultan's head.

He was too late. Sultan's body evaporated into a black mist.

"You fools," Sultan laughed, as he reappeared as a shadow on the other side of the room. "You'll never leave here alive."

"Why are you doing this?" Ismail shouted. "The candle-maidens said you'd help us."

Sultan scoffed. "Those old hags. They are out of touch with the real world of Amer. They will die. I have seen it."

Nimra pulled an arrow from her quiver and shot it at the shadow, but it passed through the mist and bounced off the wall on the other side.

Sultan laughed again. "Keep fighting," he said. "It will do you no good. You will die here. The Vicar's solders and the cipher are already coming. You will die soon, if I am merciful to you, but if not, you will be tortured first. Would you like to have a choice?"

Sultan moved closer to Ismail. With each step, the shadow seemed larger, filling the entire chamber.

And then, light as bright as day fought it back. As fast as a blink, the lion Amir appeared. The glow surrounding him filled the room with a light so bright that the shadow dispersed. Sultan stood in the corner, gaping as Amir leapt at him.

"No, no!" Sultan screamed as Amir bit his body. Amir's large paws pushed Sultan to the ground as he bit him again and again. Sultan's ancient face turned to look at Ismail. The dark power had aided him, given him long life, but even he couldn't withstand the strength of Amir. Amir was shredding him with both claws and teeth.

"Amir! Ismail yelled, but Aikiba and Nimra pulled him away from the chamber, back into the yellow light of a candle-lit corridor.

"We need to go, Ismail," Aikiba said, dragging him away from the brightness of the inner chamber. "We cannot stay here if the soldiers of Vicar come. Let's go!"

Ismail blinked, and nodded, and the group ran for the exit.

"Do you know what that thing is?" Aikiba asked as they stumbled through the outer chambers.

"Yes, that's my father's pet, Amir" said Ismail.

"Amir can use magic to tranport?" said Nimra.

"I didn't know it, either," Ismail said. "There's so much I don't know."

They slid through the hole into the courtyard, where the caged mothers waited silently and the rain fell interminably. The angry shouts of soldiers and clattering hooves of horses grew louder as the companions hid in the thick bushes hear the outer wall. A group of horsemen rode into the courtyard, and the captain shouted at his men.

"Go inside, and bring me that oath-keeper scum!"

Men dismounted and ran, as Amir roared and Sultan screamed in pain.

"Go!" Aikiba said, pushing Ismail and Nimra forward. "Keep going! Go, go!" He shoved them from behind. They stuck close to the edge of the wall, hidden by the rain and darkness and dying bushes, until they reached the courtyard gates. Then Aikiba nudged them through, and they ran toward the woods near the castle. Behind them, the castle filled with screams of dying soldiers and the roaring of Amir, who sounded angrier than ever.

CHAPTER TWENTY-FIVE – The Broken Rules, Part 1

Birds sang under the blue sky, and the white snow around the Tower of Light continued to fall and melt. The citizens of the kingdom of the north thrived in this peaceful setting. War could not come to these lands, and so peace continued.

They didn't know that inside the Tower of Light, another era of war was brewing. The three tribes of the Kingdom of the North always followed the High King's rules, and none of those rules had ever been broken. In the glowing light, two royal families stood in the chamber of the High King, drawing a plan of action.

"You want to break the rules we created?" Idun said. "You have gone mad over the times."

King Alm glanced up from the map on the table in front of him and studied Idun's face. "But my madness might save your son, Idun. We can send the elder of the Golden Army to the city of Mik-Mag to help those that are there. Their skills are unmatched in our lands, and they will give our young armies a great boost. I'll also send my right hand, Zubair, with a small force to assist Ismail and Nimra. We cannot afford to let them fail, or all of us will be dead by the end of this age."

Idun broke his gaze away from Alms' eyes and looked around the room. Beyond the fine tables, Meltôriel stood beside a window enjoying the songs of birds and a view of all the lands of the north.

"Meltôriel, Meltôriel, are listening to this?" said Idun to his Queen.

"Yes, I think Alm is right," said Meltôriel. Her matter-of-fact words clashed with her soft voice, and Idun looked momentarily surprised. "He tells the truth," she said. "If Ismail and Nimra fail in this quest, then the Cursed One will advance to the Golden Gates with a force that we have never seen before."

"She understands, so why don't you, Idun?" asked Alm. "But it matters not whether you understand. We need to act fast and send the rest of the Golden Army. If my son dies then we all die, and we cannot let this happen."

King Alm and Idun glared at each other, but neither had time to speak again. In a blinding flash of light, the great lion appeared. At the sight of blood on Amir's fur, King Alm's face paled, and his lips trembled angrily as he spoke.

"What happened?" he asked.

Amir looked at him gravely, but he made no reply. Finally, King Alm turned to Idun and Meltôriel. "Can you please excuse us?" he asked.

"Of course, High King," said Meltôriel, and the Qazam royals left the chamber. As Idun closed the door behind him, he whispered to Meltôriel. "What's up with all that blood?"

King Alm glared at Idun's back as he disappeared, and then he turned to Amir. "Now tell me what happened," he said.

"That rotten scholar Sultan betrayed us," said Amir. "He attempted to trap Ismail and Nimra—"

"I knew we should not trust a scholar!" yelled Alm. His voice reverberated throughout the tower. "Did you kill him? If not, I will go to that castle and destroy everything."

"Calm down, Alm," Amir said. "Ismail and Nimra were able to escape, but we have a bigger problem now."

"A bigger problem than that Scholar?" Alm blinked and rubbed a hand across his face.

"The Vicar," Amir said, and Alm stumbled, falling hard on the table he stood beside. He gripped it for support.

"The Vicar. How did he survive?" Shock creased King Alm's face, and his hands tightened on the edge of the table until his knuckles grew white.

"That monster shall stay far away from my son," he said. "I'll stop him myself. The last time he showed up in the lands was, you know—"

"I know, but you cannot leave past the Golden Gates," Amir said. "Things are worse than I thought. The castle was destroyed. Boys hung from the wall, and the black clouds spread in the Widow

Woods. You know that the spiders who live there will fall under the Cursed One's spell."

"This not what you saw in your vision," Alm fumed. "We should have sent Umar to the castle, rather than the Middle-lands, but the Vicar...we cannot let him live. If we do, he'll spread this curse faster than we can prepare, or worse, he will take my son and torture him. We need to help Ismail now!"

Alm rushed out of the chamber. In his hurry, he passed Idun and Meltôriel, who had heard his shouting and now stood, shocked into stillness, in the center of the corridor.

"So, the Vicar lived," said Idun, as he and Meltôriel began following him. "Are we going to the castle?"

"This whole situation seems odd, like we made a mistake," said Alm as they tried to keep up with him.

"Mistake?" Idun's voice rose. "A mistake? Our son is out there."

Alm whirled around sharply. "My sons are out there, too!" he yelled. "Do not for a second think that I'm acting like I do not care for your son, too. You have a choice. You can either help, or you can leave."

Idun sighed. "I don't like it, but I know you're right to fight this evil," said Idun. "We shall work together."

"Good. Let's go see Zubair."

Alm strode off again, with Idun and Meltôriel close behind him.

As they neared the captain's office, all the elder soldiers, whose sons were now fighting in the Middle-lands, straightened. King Alm strode into the room, and all the soldiers stood. A few whispered. "I never thought I would see the High King here!"

"Zubair!" Alm called. "Zubair!"

"My High King, how may we be a help to you and to the Qazam royal family?" asked Zubair.

"We got word from beyond the Golden Gates, and we need to send more soldiers to assist Umar in the Middle-lands," King Alm said. "Get your soldiers geared up and ready to march south to the assist the Golden Army."

"But, my High King, what about the three rules of the Golden Gates?" asked Zubair. King Alm walked closer to him. "The Vicar is alive," he said.

An immediate gasp rose from the soldiers. "I thought he died in the far east, in the Lands of the Unknown," someone said.

"Enough," the High King snapped. "You know the Vicar is a big issue for us, but even worse, he's not far from the Widow Woods. The black clouds are spreading from the Castle into the woods. That is less than a week's ride from the gates!"

"What exactly would you like us to do, my King?" Zubair said, and all the soldiers leaned forward to listen.

"We need to split the elder Golden Army into three groups," King Alm said. "A few thousand will go to the Middle-lands. Another few thousands will guard the Golden Gates. Zubair, you and the Golden Guards go to the castle and find Ismail and Nimra. When you do, you must help them in their task, in any way that you can."

He paused, looking around the room at the serious faces of the soldiers around him. "You all know this darkness, and I know many of you can never forget it," he said, "But you know this task is the only way for our kin to survive."

Zubair knelt before the High King. "My King, I feel I would be more of help to the soldiers who are marching into the Middle-lands," he said. "If you let me lead them, I promise you I'll fight until my last breath."

Alm watched Zubair for a long moment, as if he knew he might never see the face of his friend again. However, the quest held much danger no matter which direction he was sent.

"Rise, Abdulaziz," the High King said finally. "It is as you wish. You shall lead your soldiers to the Middle-lands, and we'll send the Golden Guards to the Castle of Blayney."

He lifted his voice so that all of the soldiers could hear him once more. "My kin," he said. "This war needs to stop before darkness comes to our Golden Gates to steal our light. The light from this tower must never end, or the world of Amer will be in darkness forever. Worse than that, the light inside each of us will die, and the curse will take us. Remember, we shall see each other again in the Beyond. Such is our fate, my kin, but with our sacrifices, our families will be protected. I promise you this."

He tried to keep a steady face, but it was a fight to keep back the tears. As he looked at the soldiers standing around the room, he understood that some of them would fall, because for some of them, the curse had already taken hold. This would surely lead them to their deaths.

CHAPTER TWENTY-SIX –
The Unknown Danger

Saint Lawrence marched northward at the head of his army. The dark-armored soldiers carried long spears and black shields. There were many of them...Saint Lawrence smiled as he looked over his shoulder at his army. The massive ranks were a shadow on the ground, while above them, the black clouds twisted, pouring out rain and a curse that brought despair to the hearts of men.

On the road to the city of Mik-Mag, all life had already been burned out of the land. There were no plants or trees. Anything left that could have grown were trampled by Asward riders, mounted on the same big spiders that attacked the young princes in the last battle.

Spiders were such curious creatures. Besides their voracious hunger, they were greedy. The gold, gems and wealth of men filled them with motivation that the Saint had rarely seen in other dark animals.

The Ragrok was, perhaps, the only beast that felt more passion for battle than the spiders. He slid on the ground like an oversized snake. Since the end of the Golden Age, this monster hadn't been seen in the Middle-lands. Ibies had chosen this blood-sucker particularly from a long line of ragroks. He sent it and many of its kin north to bring fear to the Norms—and these creatures did. They weren't motivated by wealth, as the spiders were. They sought only blood.

They would have their blood, and the spiders would have their wealth. As far as Saint Lawrence himself, capturing the princes would mean more favors and more respect from Ibies.

Ingie trotted up to the saint. "Saint Lawrence, the Asward scouts ahead of us can see the gates of the city," he said. "What are your orders?"

Saint Lawrence smiled. "I have only one plan," he said. "Send in the Ragrok first."

Ingie's eyes widened, and the soldiers immediately behind him glanced at each other in fear. No one had seen the Ragrok unleashed in years.

"As you command, my Saint," said Ingie.

"Oh, Ingie, I have not forgotten that you failed to take the princes with Hassen during your first attack. Be thinking about this, and be expecting for your consequences back at the tower," said the saint.

Ingie shifted uncomfortably. "Yes, my Saint," he said, and he quickly road to the Asward scouts and to the other captains, sharing the orders. It was difficult to keep his mind on the task, because he kept thinking about what might be in store for him back at the slaughter-house.

The Saint turned again, watching the Ragrok. The Ragrok slid quietly, leaving a trail of sticky yellow fluid.

"You know what to do, Ragrok," the saint said. "Once we get closer to the gates, kill anything that moves, but bring no harm to the princes. Leave them alive for Ibies," said the Saint.

The beast nodded his head in agreement, but he didn't really care about the princes anyway. All he wanted was blood to quench his thirst.

Horns blew. Drums beat. Inside the city, Norms shrieked and ran for their best hiding places. In times such as these, no one wanted to be in the line of sight for such an army. The Saint had no fears of any backlash from the city of Mik-Mag. They had already lost everything in the past. He doubted they could or would put up a fight. At least, it wouldn't be much of a fight. Ibies' forces would trample them into the ground.

The pure black clouds reached the gates of the city, and the citizens felt the ground shake. A rumbling filled the air, growing louder by the second.

The Saint smiled. His army would be at the gates in only a few minutes, but already the attack had begun. The Ragrok beast's long body slid over the walls of the city, already biting every moving thing it saw. Screams rose inside the city walls.

The Saint halted, waving his army to a standstill.

"Shall we help it?" asked a soldier near the saint.

"No," Saint Lawrence said. "Let the Ragrok take care of this. His thirst will kill anything he lays sees, and only a fool would try to stop a Ragrok when he's been given the promise of blood."

The prince and the Golden Army, who were camping on the far side of the city, jumped to their feet when the first screams pierced the air. They rushed in and out of tents, grabbing their armor and yelling orders at each other. None were ready for such an untimely attack.

Umar emerged from his tent in full armor. The long red cape he wore swung from his shoulders and his face was stern.

"Za-Lamir! Line up!" he called. He jumped onto the back of his horse, and his cavalry began forming a single line behind him. Kaf and Adn slipped in right behind his horse, ready to fight. Umar's heart felt hot. After the deaths of so many of his kin, he was ready to fight back.

"Everyone, stay on your guard!" he called. "Do not let your brothers riding next to you down. Do not blink if you have the chance to swing your sword, and do not run away when your brothers are dying. May God protect us and drive this evil from these lands!"

"Amen," replied the soldiers with one unanimous shout. Once the stragglers joined the ranks, Umar led them forward toward the city. They heard screams.

"What's going on in there?" Adn's words were tight with fear.

"I do not know, my brother, but we shall find out soon enough," Umar said. "Be on your guard and do not fear to kill anyone who might bring harm to our kin."

Adn looked at his elder brother. He took in the harsh set of his chin, the serious tone in his voice and the anger in his eyes. In this dark time, Umar had become bloodthirsty or at least he hungered for revenge.

Kaf caught Adn's eyes. He seemed worried about Umar, too, but there was no time to think about it now. Kaf held his bow tight and turned his attention to the road in front of them. The Golden Army reached the city, where blood already flowed at the edge of the streets. The bodies of dead Norms were scattered throughout the area, but there was no sign of the dark-armored soldiers they had fought before.

"There are bodies and blood and more bodies, but where are the soldiers?" someone said in a low, fearful voice. "Maybe something else caused this destruction. What's that yellow slime everywhere?"

At Umar's command, the Golden Soldiers split up to look around for any sign of their enemies. They had barely broken apart when the Ragrok slid from a rooftop onto a mounted soldier. The horse fell, and the soldier screamed as the Ragrok bit deep.

The Ragrok worked quickly. "No!" screamed another Golden Soldier as the Ragrok pulled him off of his horse.

"What is that!" shouted Adn. The Ragrok beast lunged at him from the side of a nearby wall. Adn dodged and struck hard with his sword, but the beast's skin was as hard as a rock.

"The sword does not hurt it," he yelled. "Go for its eyes!"

The Golden Soldiers surrounded the beast, jabbing at it as it bit and slashed at the soldiers. They fought bravely, attacking it again and again as Kaf climbed the wall above the Ragrok. While he was distracted by one of the soldiers, Kaf jumped from the wall onto its back. The Ragrok was all scales, so it was hard to hold on, but Kaf held tight, moving slowly toward the beast' head. With every step, he dug deep between the scales with his sword. The beast roared in anger and pain, but Kaf reached his head and jammed his sword into the Ragrok's left eye.

The beast roared again as green blood began to flow from where its eye had been.

On the plains outside the city, Saint Lawrence frowned. "Something is wrong," he said. "Send in the rest of the soldiers."

While they rushed forward, the Golden Army still fought the Ragrok. Its screams made some of the soldiers cover their ears. The beast stomped and lashed, killing a few of the Golden Soldiers purely by accident. Then Adn called out another warning.

"Spiders!"

The Golden Soldiers spun around just in time to see the Asward soldiers on their spiders, climbing over the city walls.

"Za-Lamir! Line up!" yelled Umar. The soldiers immediately moved into position, holding their golden shields and swords.

The spiders only saw the gold. "Give me gold!" they shrieked. "Give it to us!"

" Za-Jaa! Charge!" yelled Umar. All at once, the Golden Soldiers rushed forward toward the Asward riders. On the far side of the city, the Northern Kin in the rear of the Golden Army shouted as the gates behind them creaked open. Dark soldiers poured through, striking fear into the hearts of the Golden Soldiers, but they pushed on.

The soldiers yelled as they ran forward toward the dark soldiers, swords swinging. The battle for the city of Mik-Mag had begun once more.

It was fierce. Swords clashed into shields, arrows flew, and bodies began piling up in the streets. In spite of their inexperience, the Golden Soldiers were holding their own this time. Kaf and Adn fought side by side, keeping their focus by laughing and making fun of the dark-armored soldiers. At times, they battled five enemies at once.

On the other side of the battle, the darkness in Umar was growing. Rather than keeping his composure, anger filled his heart, and he swung with reckless precision. A spider, hungry for his Golden Armor, attacked him, striking at him with long, sharp legs. Umar struck back, slicing the legs off the spider one by one. He turned toward his fellow soldiers, who were falling under the spiders as quickly as they had during the first battle.

"Attack the spiders!" he yelled, hoping that fewer spiders would ease the battle for them. He attacked another spider, jabbing even faster at its underbelly and legs. After taking down a few more spiders, Kaf discovered the spiders had no direction without their riders on top of them. When he shot the riders with arrows, the spiders fled away.

Kaf and Umar teamed up. Umar attacked the spider's eyes, while Kaf took down the riders on top. In spite of their progress, the armies of Saint Lawrence pressed further into the city. With the presence of Saint Lawrence, the dark clouds and rain magnified the deep sense of hopelessness and despair that the Northern Kin felt. Their only thoughts now were thoughts of failure, or worse—what if they weren't worthy for this task?

The princes and the Golden Army fought on, but Saint Lawrence's force surrounded them. There was no escape. In the midst of the battle, the one-eyed ragrok still loomed, lashed, and fed.

Somehow, the last Asward soldier had fallen, and the spiders were gone. In a brief moment of victory, Prince Umar looked around, smiling at his remaining kin.

It wasn't enough. The fighting paused as a young man with long white hair and a spotless white robe approached. He grinned and laughed.

"You think killing those pawns was the end of your troubles, young princes," Saint Lawrence said. "This is a delightful day. Let darkness rain down on this glorious day! The only way you can ever survive this is if you give up now. If not, the rest of your soldiers will die here in this forgotten land of Norms. It is only you, the three princes, that we are after." He pointed at Umar, Adn, and Kaf in return, and his voice rang proudly in the bloodied streets.

Rage filled Umar's face. He stomped past his soldiers and over the dead bodies of a spider and its fallen rider.

"Come get us!" he yelled, pulling up his sword for another round of fighting.

The Saint laughed merrily. "You heard him, boys. Get those princes, and kill everyone else. Leave no prisoners." His insane laughter overtook him again, and he withdrew from the battle, which had begun with vigor once again.

As the dark-armored soldiers moved in for the kill, the Ragrok slid through the battle, grabbing Golden Soldiers one by one. The princes stood their ground, but their kin around them died without hope or help. Arrows bounced off the golden shields but pierced their kin fighting nearby. Dark spears stabbed behind he shields, causing many Golden Soldiers to fall from their horses, where they were trampled by other warriors.

They were unable to hold their lines any longer. The princes pushed forward, fighting with all their might, while their kin fell behind them.

One young kin screamed as a spear in his side toppled him to the ground. Even with the commotion around him, Umar's attention was drawn to the young man. He killed another dark soldier and ran to the side of his dying kin.

"My brother, are you going to be okay?" Umar asked.

"Ah, my prince! May God help us!" The light went out of the young soldier's eyes as he passed away.

Not two steps away, another of his kin fell.

"My prince," the young Golden Soldier gasped, as blood dripped from the side of his mouth. "I'm sorry."

"My brother, please do not leave us!" yelled Umar. His voice broke as the light faded from the face of his kin.

"Tell my father I was too weak to come back," the young soldier gasped. "I will miss the Tower of Light."

"No!" yelled Umar, grabbing the body of his fallen kin. Tears of grief and anger mingled with the rain on his face.

In that moment, a horn blew loudly from the north. The sound of galloping horses and yelling soldiers grew louder, until King Duncan and Prince Sumer appeared with their armies at the top of the hill outside the city.

They paused only for a moment, taking in the smoke, the darkness, and the screams. King Duncan's face paled, but he yelled in his loudest voice.

"You run now, you scum!"

The northern armies charged forward in massive numbers, passing citizens who were fleeing the city toward the West Road.

While the fresh northern armies approached, the princes and their remaining men still fought. The Ragrok crawled along the walls at the edge of the city, nearer to the princes, who were showing signs of fatigue. Their swings weren't as quick, and their aim wasn't as precise as it had been.

Qazam soldiers climbed to the tops of the buildings, shooting arrows into the dark soldiers over the prince's heads. It was an enormous boost. Prince Umar took the opportunity to rally his troops once more.

"For the High King!" he yelled, running past his soldiers toward the line of dark-armored soldiers in front of him. Behind him, all the Golden Soldiers followed, and the fresh armies took up the battle in the rear.

"Kill them all," said Saint Lawrence calmly, while the Norms of the north burst through the gates and overtook his own forces. The large size of the northern Norms, their heavy steel weapons and their large numbers, combined with the Qazam's skill and accuracy, finally began to overpower the dark soldiers.

Saint Lawrence looked over the battle. It was a lost cause now. He would lose most of his forces, but he didn't intend to leave empty-handed. What would Ibies say, or worse, what would he do, if the Saint failed? It wasn't a thought he cared to contemplate.

"Ragrok, grab those filthy princes, and let's leave this bloodbath," he called. Sharp anger filled his voice. As the Ragrok swung around, he surveyed the situation. None of the Asward soldiers had survived, and hundreds of his other soldiers lay dead or dying in the middle of the battle.

The Ragrok was as cunning as he was dangerous. He crept behind the Golden Army. Kaf and Adn fought on horseback near a house with one wall left standing. As they swung their swords toward the dark soldiers in front of them, the Ragrok lunged its neck forward, through the large broken window. He bit both princes on their legs, clasping tight to them. He retreated with such force that the princes slipped from their horses and were pulled back through the window.

Umar saw this. "No, you beast!" he yelled, striking the Ragrok's thick skin with his sword.

The sword couldn't penetrate the Ragrok's scales. Nothing he did stopped the beast from sliding forward, carrying his brothers with him.

"Get this beast now!" Umar thundered, fighting back the dark soldiers who attacked him. With his eyes wide open, Umar pushed the dark soldiers back. Three of them fell with one swing of his blade. His anger boiled. He turned to another soldier, readying for another strike. His blood-lust was so strong...

"My Prince, stop!" yelled one of his kin from behind of him. "We must get your brothers back!"

Umar blinked and nodded, running toward the Ragrok again. The beast slid close to Saint Lawrence, who waited in calm, cold anger by the Southern Gates. The Saint looked with disdain on his dead and dying soldiers, who meant nothing to him, and nodded at the Ragrok.

"Good. Take those scum to the tower now!"

The massive Ragrok slid out of the city, making an unpleasant squishing sound as he rolled over slices of wood and broken stones. Inside his mouth, Kaf and Adn choked and grasped their legs, trying to free themselves enough to fight their way free. It was no use. The Ragrok's poison overtook them, and they faded into an unpleasant sleep.

"Stop that beast!" Umar yelled, pushing through the soldiers who stood in front of him. "Get him!"

The battle was still too fierce for Umar to break through. Although he continuously fought, although his sword was covered in blood, although his eyes were wide and his hair matted from the rain, he could make no progress forward. When he did, he had to climb over dead bodies and limbs from fallen spiders, avoiding the Ragrok's green blood and sticky yellow slime.

At the edge of the city, the saint watched Umar's desperate attempts to reach him. He noticed the bloodlust and wondered if he should kill him—but what was the point now? Saint Lawrence knew he had what he wanted from this blood bath. He slowly pulled his forces back. They fled through the Southern Gates.

Umar looked over at the Saint, whose robes of white were still spotless.

"You monster!" he yelled. "You have done this!"

"This has been fun," the Saint said, grinning. "Will you remember me? And say hello to your father for me. Sadly, I must go now."

The Saint turned and rode out of the city. Umar lunged forward again, but his way was blocked by the remaining dark soldiers.

Only a few of the Golden Soldiers remained, fighting side by side with Umar.

"Do not let that monster of a man go!" said Umar, slashing at another dark soldier.

"My prince, we can't reach him," said Zuda. Pure fear filled his voice.

"They took my brothers! We need to get them back!" Umar whirled around, seeking more help, but all he saw was death. The bodies of his close kin lay scattered on the ground. Their golden attire was covered with mud and ashes.

Umar had failed them all.

"What have I done?" he whispered the words, but they sounded like torrents in his own ears as he looked in disgust on the battlefield. He watched, weary and heartsick, as the last of the soldiers of the Saint fled the city or were killed by Norms and Qazams.

King Duncan rode to Prince Umar's side.

"My Prince, I am sorry that we were not able to get here earlier," he said. "There is so much death and darkness in this place. Does anyone know why they came here, and what that beast was?"

Duncan slid off his horse and began ordering men around. Qazam soldiers moved in to tend to the wounded, while Norms began clearing the streets of debris and bodies or helping citizens who had been trapped in their homes. Several soldiers were dispatched to block the broken gates.

He turned back to Prince Umar as Prince Sumer stepped up beside them.

"I have never seen this much death," Sumer said. "I don't know how to handle this." Shock and pain filled his face, but it was nothing compared to the despair that Umar felt. He thought only about his brothers, and the dark curse settled into his bones.

"Why did they attack this city?" Duncan asked.

"Because of us." Umar spoke quickly, and his voice was faded and tinny. "They wanted to get the princes. But why are the Qazam and Norm armies here?"

"We were sent from you're the High King," said Sumer.

"Ah, he knew we needed help," Umar said. "He knew before I could have sent him a seal." He looked over the battlefield once more. "The way things are going, we might not be going home for a very long time," he said.

He walked away, toward the tents of the Northern Kin. Many of them would be empty now. Some would have a few soldiers left, who were now helping with the wounded and retrieving golden swords from the streets and peeling golden armor from dead bodies.

All of the tents would be filled with grief and pain. Rain and blood would still flow through the city streets while the dark clouds circled around it from above.

CHAPTER TWENTY-SEVEN –
Vicar of Terror

Fearsome bolts of lightning flashed in the clouds, and thunder boomed. Rain poured from the sky, drenching the mothers who cried in their cages outside the Castle of Blayney. Below them, the Vicar and his soldiers filled the courtyard, looking for clues about the whereabouts of the oath-keeper.

The Vicar strode past the bodies of dead soldiers, into the castle and through the fine rooms, now in shambles. At the inner chamber, he called to Sultan and found him, struggling for breath, in the far corner.

"Ah, you're still alive, I see," said the Vicar as he stood in the doorway. His slim body barely filled the doorframe, but he looked ominous just the same. His long nails and boney hands twitched as he watched Sultan try to sit up. The wounds from Amir's attack were too severe.

"Help," Sultan gasped. "Help me! You gave me this power. You can save me!"

"I'm not here to save you, Sultan the Scholar," the Vicar said. "You failed in the one task that I assigned to you!" The Vicar's voice was calm, but cold. He stepped forward into the room, peering down at Sultan as he spoke again. "You have permission to tell me what happened and how the oath-scum got away. If you can tell me where he might be heading, I might even forgive you. I am in a good mood, after all."

Sultan tried to laugh, but it was too painful. "Amir came and attacked me," he panted. "That beast has such strength, even in his old age. He also killed your soldiers outside. Such anger he has! But the oath-keeper and his companions escaped during the fight."

"Interesting," the Vicar said. "The oath-scum is not alone? And Amir coming this far from the gate is such a dangerous move. This might be the basis for a new plan."

Sultan spit blood as he coughed and tried to speak again. "The oath-keeper was with a knight from the West-lands and a Qazam girl," he said. "Now I have told you everything that I know. Help me!"

"Like I said, Sultan, I'm not here to help you," the Vicar said. "I'll find this oath-scum and his friends even if I have to send my cipher far into the West-lands, but you'll die here, as will those mothers that you betrayed."

He turned away, but then turned back, as if seeking to reassure the Scholar.

"Remember when you came to me, by the Desert of Khalif? You begged me for water, like a dog. I gave you power and trained you in shadow magic, but for what? A weak cloth of flesh, flesh that my dogs would love to eat. You see, they haven't eaten a good meal in days."

The Vicar snapped his fingers, and two demon dogs entered the chamber as he left it. Sultan's screams reached the castle courtyard, but by the time the Vicar exited into the rain, they had died away.

Soldiers still searched along the edges of the courtyard, and ciphers, like misty shadows, walked the grounds in the distance.

"He's not there," said the Vicar to Valerian, the leader of the soldiers.

"My Vicar, we can raid any nearby villages to see if they might have come across those scum," said Valerian, running his hands through his short hair. The large scar near his left eye seemed to stand out in the rain.

The Vicar looked away. "No, that will be not needed," he said. "Bring me the mothers from inside these cages. Maybe they have seen them. Send me my dogs, also."

He walked back inside the castle as the soldiers unlocked the cages and pulled the mothers out into the courtyard.

"Please leave us be!" said one mother.

"Get out now!" said the soldier, yanking the mother forward and forcing her into the castle.

"Please let us go!" another mother screamed, and the courtyard was once again filled with shrieks and cries.

"Move, move!" Valerian said. "Go into the castle now!"

The last of the mothers was pulled inside, deep into the chambers, where the Vicar was sitting in a chair. The soldiers in the room lit candles, so the fine paintings, golden tables and red carpet of the past were plainly visible.

"Come inside, ladies," the Vicar said. "Come sit. Sit, please."

The mothers sat, terrified, looking wide-eyed both at the Vicar and at the doorway of the inner chamber, where a pool of blood could be seen.

"What do you want from us?" one woman cried. "You already took everything thing from us!"

"Shh," the Vicar said. "I'll be the one asking questions tonight. Some of you might know why we are here. You might have seen a boy, someone you hope will restore your freedom, but you are mistaken. All your sons lay dead, and your husbands are dead, just like your hope."

He stood and walked around the room, circling the scared women, who huddled together in the center. In the yellow light, his face looked waxy and pale, and his lips were as red as the carpet.

"Now," he said. "Who knows where that oath-scum went? Does anyone want to talk?"

From the far corner, the demon dogs stalked forward. They bared their teeth and circled the floor, just as the Vicar had done. Their long bodies smelled of death, and their eyes glowed red.

"Please, we do not know anything," whispered Mehreen. "Please, leave us in peace."

"Peace," said the Vicar, walking quickly to Mehreen's side. "You think you can have peace. What is your name?"

"I'm Mehreen," she replied in a thick, terrified whisper.

"Mehreen, what gives you the hope to say something like the word peace?" The Vicar's voice was cold and angry.

Something broke inside Mehreen.

"You will not take our hope away," she said, still shaking. "You have taken our sons, our husbands, and our homes, but you cannot take our hope."

Under the Vicar's scrutiny, she looked down, and the Vicar started to laugh.

"You must have seen that oath-scum, Mehreen, or you would not talk like that," he said. "Did you? Tell me now, or my demon dogs will eat every mother in this room."

"I don't know anything," Mehreen said. "Please, stop this."

The vicar looked at his demon dogs. They lunged forward, biting one mother on her leg and another on her arm. The women screamed in pain.

"Stop it, now!" cried Mehreen.

"Tell me what I need to know, Mehreen, and this will be over," said the Vicar.

"Fine! Just stop!" Mehreen yelled.

The Vicar looked at his demon dogs. The released the women and slunk back into the corner.

"You women are lucky," the Vicar said. "If Mehreen wasn't here, you would all surely be dead."

He turned to Mehreen. "Now, tell me all that you know."

"There were three of them, all dressed in black," she whispered. "The oath-keeper's name was Ismail."

"Ismail," the Vicar said. "Ismail. That name. What about the Qazam girl?"

"I don't know," Mehreen said. "She did not say anything to me. Please, that's all I know."

"Fine," the vicar said, nodding. "I hope you feel proud of telling me this information. Valerian, put these ladies back into their cages and cut Mehreen's tongue out." He turned back to Mehreen and smiled as he left the room. "I hope this teaches you something," he said.

"Please, no!" cried Mehreen as Valerian grabbed her. "Please, no!"

Soldiers surrounded the other women and yanked them to their feet, forcing them back into their cages in the courtyard. The Vicar emerged, followed by Valerian, who was wiping the blade of his knife against his leg.

"Valerian, get the soldier's ready," the vicar said. "With this new information, we'll need to ride a little bit into the West-lands. It's going to be a long ride. Bring me some of the demon dogs."

"Of course, my Vicar, but what about the cipher?" asked Valerian.

"Hmm. Send them to wander around the area here. Let them feed off the noir from the Norms. They haven't been fed for weeks, maybe even months—but tell them to alert us if they see anything."

The Vicar mounted his horse and rode past Mehreen, who sat in a cage in the outer courtyard now. He nodded almost pleasantly as he passed her.

"If I come back here to this rotted castle, you'll be the first one I'll hang," he said. Lightning flashed again as he rode off into the dark rain.

CHAPTER TWENTY-EIGHT – The Broken Rules, Part 2

The elders on the top of the wall of the Golden Gates watched as the elder army marched past below.

"What is the world of Amer coming to?" asked Jud. "First the Golden Army, then the Norms and the Qazams, and now the elders of the Northern Kin?"

"Yes," an ancient elder said in return. "The darkness is growing faster than we can feel it. Even the city of Mik-Mag is now filled with it. When I reach out, it's as if Ibies is touching my skin. If I reach west, near the Castle of Blayney, I feel an evil Norm spreading his curse deep into the Widow Woods. The Northern Kin heading there might have a fight on their hands."

As he rubbed the cloth covering his eyes, Jud spoke again.

"This is breaking the rules of these gates," he said.

"I agree, but we cannot let this curse spread far into our lands, or we will become like the Lands of the Unknown in the far east. This same curse spread there like a wildfire, causing Norms to turn mad, forgetful and hateful. Some just walked away into the woods and never came back. Even worse, some learned to thrive on the misfortunes of others. We cannot stand by and let this happen to us. If it means breaking our own rules, so be it."

The ancient elder and Jud both nodded in agreement, but below them, King Idun was still uneasy about the idea. He sat atop his horse, next to King Alm, as horsemen clopped by, following Zubair down the road toward Mik-Mag.

"Are you sure about this, High King?" asked Idun.

"What do you mean?" said King Alm, watching the light of the north spread into the South-lands, taking in the final moment of his friends and kin riding away. No one knew whether they would see each other again.

"What do I mean?" Idun flared. "What about the fact that we broke the rules and allowed those tainted soldiers back into the darkness of the curse?"

"Watch yourself, Idun. What do you know about being tainted by the darkness?" said Alm. "Like I said in the Tower of Light, this action will help both of us. Don't be so irked about it."

"You will see that no good will come out of this, my High King," said Idun bitterly. He galloped away, and Meltôriel rode with him, although she looked over her shoulder at the High King once.

"This is the right action, Alm," said Amir, stepping forward into the light. "Do not relive the past too much."

King Alm rubbed his beard with his hand. "How do we really know?" he said. "I feel that something bad has already happened, but I feel so helpless to aid my own sons and our kin."

The gate slowly started to close, although the sounds of golden boots on a barren road could still be heard.

"Do you still want to do this?" asked Amir. Alm nodded in agreement.

"As you wish," said Amir. Alm held tight to Amir's golden fur, and in a flash of light, they disappeared from outside the Golden Gates and reappeared inside the candle-maidens cave.

"Oh, look, it's the oath-breaker and his trusted pet!" One of the maidens laughed.

"We have an entryway, or did you forget?" said Marta, setting off another peel of laughter in her companions. "How may we help you, High King of the north?"

"We have not come here for jokes," Alm said quietly. "You know what you did. You forced my son into an early death."

"Oh, I see," said Marta. "You think this oath that your son took upon himself is a death sentence? If so, why are you still alive and walking around? Why is this curse still spreading, bringing darkness and death to all the children around the world of Amer? They have been dying for hundreds of years now. If you had done what we asked you to do in the first place, no one would be in this predicament now. Your eldest sons would not be battling in the Middle-lands, and Ismail would not be heading to the Western Kingdom."

"You sent Ismail to the West Kingdom," Alm said, "Where a mad king sits upon the throne. Have you gone mad, or are you just too comfortable in this cave?"

He stepped forward, holding out both hands in a pleading gesture. His voice grew both rough and soft. "Just tell me what this quest is and I'll go fulfill it," he said.

"You?" snorted another candle-maiden.

"She's right," said Marta. "You can't fulfill the oath now. You are tainted. You have a darkness in you, and we feel it. My guess is that even the elder watchers feel it, too, but they're too afraid to say anything to you. If they did, you might walk past those gates. Once the dark clouds spread over you again, you'd be lost and you would never return. Please, tell me that I'm wrong. Tell me that you have not felt this darkness in you."

King Alm bowed his head. "You know I cannot say that," he said. "But I'm just a father trying to save his sons. I'll do whatever I can for them, and you should remember this: if anything happens to Ismail, nothing in the northern lands could save you from me."

Marta laughed, and the candle-maidens sat around their table, never moving.

CHAPTER TWENTY-NINE – The Land of Mystery

Aikiba led Ismail and Nimra away from the Castle of Blayney. They ran fast, but the demon dogs of the Vicar howled in the distance. Laenatan was nowhere to be seen.

"Keep going," Aikiba said. "This way, and keep your heads down!"

"I think they're getting closer to us," Nimra said, trying to catch her breath. "I keep hearing dogs, but they do not sound like normal dogs. We need to find a place to hide."

"Demon dogs" said Aikiba, and inside his helmet, his eyebrows crinkled with worry. "Those might be Vicar's demon dogs. You're right. We need to hide if we have any hope of surviving tonight. Let's head into those woods. Maybe we'll find someplace that will mask our scent."

"Wait," Nimra asked. "What are demon dogs?"

"I'll explain that to you if we live!" said Aikiba, "Now run! We don't have time for questions!"

He led them into the woods, but before they could move far, something caught Ismail's attention.

"Is that my father?" He looked up, toward the top of a little hill, where a shadow stood, surrounded by mist, only a few yards away.

Ismail smiled and started forward, but Aikiba pulled him back. "Wait, what?" He looked up at the shadow. He grew white and dropped to the ground.

"It's a cipher," he said. "Get down! Now!"

"But it's my father," Ismail said happily. "If he looks down, he might see us and help us."

"That's not your father, Ismail!" Aikiba said. "It's a cipher. It will change into whatever you want to see. Please, get down before it calls for reinforcement."

"Nimra, tell him," said Ismail, but Nimra stood quietly. She also gazed at the cipher, blinking as if she couldn't believe what she saw.

Both of you, get down!" Aikiba hissed, and he grabbed them by their elbows and pulled them to the ground.

"Why did you do that, Aikiba?" Ismail said, trying to stand again. "It's my father!"

"Listen to me!" Aikiba said. "That's not your father. Why would he be standing at the top of that hill, but not looking at you? It's because ciphers are able to change into any form. They always choose a form that draws people to it, so they can feed on them. We need to act fast and move away before that cipher finds us."

"But it felt real," said Ismail. "I saw my father, but he wasn't looking at me."

Nimra touched his arm, patting it as she spoke. "I saw my father, too, but Aikiba is right. My father died a long time ago. That's how I know it could not have been your father, Ismail. Come now. Let's move quickly."

Ismail took a deep breath. "You're right. That thing—it wasn't able to recreate my father's light. If it could have, how would we be able to tell if it was a cipher or not?"

"There's no time for questions like that," said Aikiba. "Let's go this way. These woods might lead to the West-lands."

They crawled forward through the brush until they were certain that the mists and the cipher were behind them. Then they stood and ran westward. As in the Widow Woods, the light in this forest faded the deeper they went, and the trees were thick and tall. However, this forest had a bit of life left. The leaves were still a yellowish green.

"Do you hear birds?" asked Nimra, and they listened to faint bird sounds as they ran between the tree trunks.

"I haven't heard any birds since we left the Golden Gates," Ismail said, "But that reminds me. I hope Laenatan is okay," said Ismail.

"I bet he's fine," said Nimra. "How many birds do you know of his size?"

Ismail laughed. "Not many, but I still have my worries about him. He's never been in these places, either. I don't want him to get lost."

"Like us," said Aikiba, and he sounded cautious. "These woods are not like the Widow Woods. That forest is dark and cursed, but these woods have some sounds of life in it. Still, we must be careful to stay together and stay on our course."

It was difficult to move forward quickly in the darkness. Only a little light broke through the dark clouds above the forest, and most of that didn't filter down to the forest floor. Ismail and Nimra followed Aikiba, listening to the echoing songs of birds and something like deer or rabbits rustling in the tall bushes around them.

"Have you been here before, Aikiba?" asked Ismail.

"Well, if I was, I barely remember it. These clouds bring only evil thoughts, and nothing of my past. I don't know why it doesn't affect you."

"I don't know, either," said Ismail, "But it sounds horrible. I feel really bad for you and everyone that is affected by it. I promise you I'll find a way to stop it, although I do not yet know how or even why."

Although it was nice to see life in this forest, it was also difficult to keep up with Aikiba. He stood three times as tall as Ismail and Nimra. He stepped through the high weeds and around the thick tree roots with ease, while Ismail and Nimra hurried along behind him. When they stopped to catch their breath, Ismail looked around, panting a little.

"What was the last thing you remember, if that's okay to ask?" he said.

"Hmm. Let me think," said Aikiba. He sat down on a fallen tree trunk, trying to break through the mental fog the curse had caused in his mind.

"I was riding with my fellow knights," he said finally. His words came slowly, as if he fought to retrieve each one. "I got separated from them, and I was lost. That's when I met you."

"When I met you, you said you came from a tower close to a castle, and that you came from the West-lands," Ismail said. "Were the knights you were with from the West Kingdom, too?"

"We all had similar armor, but none of them had a helmet like mine," said Aikiba. He pinched the bridge of his nose, shaking his head slightly as if to clear the cobwebs. Then he stood, and he spoke a little more quickly. "We need to get moving again."

They pushed forward through the thick woods. There seemed to be no end in sight and although they heard animal noises, they never actually saw an animal, or even signs of it. There were no pawprints on the path in front of them, feathers in the brush, and no nests in the trees.

"This way," said a voice in the distance.

"Which way?" asked Nimra.

Both Aikiba and Ismail stopped and looked at her.

"What did you say?" they asked her in unison.

The whisper from the woods came again.

"This way."

Nimra peered into the woods, and then into the faces of her friends. "That," she said. "Did you hear that?"

"No," Aikiba said. "We only hear you, talking to yourself as if you're a crazy person."

"I hear a voice," Nimra said, furrowing her brow. "It's saying, 'This way.'"

Again, the whisper floated on the breeze.

"This way."

"I heard it again!" she said. "Please tell me you heard it." She moved closer to Ismail.

"I don't hear it," he said, and he put an arm around her shoulders. She looked confused, and maybe a little unsure of herself. "If you hear a voice, let's follow it. Lead us where the voice wants to go."

"Okay," Nimra said sharply. Concern made her face look pinched and confused. "I just don't know what might lie ahead for us."

Aikiba stepped back toward her, trampling sprigs of tall weeds to the forest floor. He put his hand on her shoulder. "I'll protect you with my life, my young Qazam," he said.

Nimra smiled. "Thank you, Aikiba. "That means a lot."

She smiled at Ismail, pulled away from her two friends, and drew her bow. As she stepped into the tall grasses, the voice came again.

"This way."

Ismail and Aikiba followed Nimra for an hour, and then another. At times, they moved straight, and other times, they went back and forth, zig-zagging and circling until they were all disoriented. They reached a place where they moved only between two trees—one on the far right of a clearing, and one on the far left. As they moved between them, the voice continued to beckon them. Nimra grew frustrated.

"I can't take it anymore," she said. "Stop saying 'This way, this way, this way.' Nothing is changing, and we're not making any progress."

Ismail stood beside her, trying to comfort her. "It's okay," he said. "We do not have to follow that voice. It could be all in your head."

He started to laugh, and Nimra turned to look at him. Her eyes widened.

"Wait!" she said. "Something in your bag is glowing. What is it?"

"I don't know," he said. "Let me take a look. Oh, it's my rusted crown. Why is it glowing?"

He held up the rusty crown, which glowed with a brilliant white light that illuminated the area around them. As the companions looked at it, plants and trees immediately started to kick back to life. The faded grass became greener, flowers bloomed, and the yellowed leaves on the trees brightened into a lush, verdant canopy.

"This kind of light hasn't been here for a long time," Aikiba said quietly.

"What does this mean?" asked Ismail.

"I don't know, but that crown is too bright for this kind of place," Aikiba said. "We do not want any unwanted attention."

Ismail moved to put the crown back in his sack when the whisper came again. "Wear it."

"Ismail, place that crown on your head," said Nimra.

"Why?" Ismail looked surprised.

"The voice told me."

Ismail swallowed his feelings of uneasiness and placed the glowing white crown, the sign of the oath-keeper, on his head. Immediately, the large tree in front of them transformed into a white tree, showering glowing sunrays throughout the woods. A set of stone stairs looped around the trunk, leading to a large house high in the forest canopy.

"Such beauty," Aikiba breathed. "It is the very light of hope, and it leaves me speechless."

"Wait," said Ismail. He removed the bright crown, and in half a breath, the tree withered into dark black with barely any signs of life. When Ismail placed the crown on his head again, the tree transformed into a heavenly tree once more.

Aikiba laughed with joy. "Have you ever seen anything like this before?" he asked.

""Yes, but only at the tower of light," Ismail said. "How is this possible?"

The whispered voice came again. Nimra smiled at Ismail and Aikiba.

"The voice is telling us to come," she said.

"Up to those stairs around the tree?" Ismail frowned in confusion, but the voice whispered gently. "Come. Come."

"Yes," Nimra said. "Let's go."

"Fine, but I'll lead," said Ismail, and he began stepping up the stairs, enjoying the view as the staircase spiraled upward. The entire tree glowed with the same white light that emanated from the tower of light.

"Are we safe to walk up in this tree?" asked Aikiba.

"What do you mean?"

"Well, think about it. We just escaped the Vicar and the Cipher and demon dogs. Now there is a voice leading us. Should we trust that mystical voice?"

"I don't trust the voice, but I trust Nimra," Ismail said. "If she thinks we should go this way, even if it's up in a tree, then we shall go this way."

"As you wish, oath-keeper," said Aikiba. He followed Ismail quietly, with Nimra trailing behind them. When they reached halfway up the trunk, a voice called down from the top of the tree.

"You there, boy," the voice said. "Have you not read the sign?"

The group stopped. Aikiba drew his great-sword, and Nimra pulled an arrow from her quiver.

"You there, boy," the voice said again. "We feel you, but this is no home for Norms or Qazams. Do you know how to speak?"

"Yes, but we only speak to someone or something within our view," said Ismail.

He looked up, and then ahead as a glowing white shadow appeared on the steps in front of him. Two white eyes floated in the center of the white mist, but there were no arms nor legs, and not even a mouth.

"Answer my question," said the white figure. "Have you not read the sign?"

"No," said Ismail, and his voice sounded small. He trembled as he spoke. "There was no sign to read."

"No sign?" The formless figure blinked. "That's interesting. Where did you get that crown?"

"This is my crown," said Ismail. "I'm the oath-keeper.

CHAPTER THIRTY – A Grand Plan

The darkness of the clouds slowly dissipated from around the city of Mik-Mag, letting enough sunlight through to turn the sky into a heavy, slate-gray color. In the city below, blood still filled the streets, but the soldiers were gathering the limbs and bodies of spiders outside the city, where they would be burned. The spiders were too big to move easily, so it took a lot of effort.

Meanwhile, the citizens of the city were trying to repair their damaged homes and the gates that the enemy soldiers had ruined. A few of them carried the bodies of fallen dark soldiers to a local graveyard, which was already overfull from decades of hard battles. Only a handful of men scoured the streets for golden attire that might have come off during the battle. These men horded such items, taking them into the market of El Dorado to be sold.

The Golden Army was few in numbers now. They gathered outside the city, near their camp, to bury their dead, who were lined up in a row. Each body was completely covered in a wrapping of white cloth. The remaining Golden Soldiers stood beside the bodies, grieving, while the Norms of the north and the Qazams formed lines behind them. Umar stood with his head bowed, barely moving.

"My prince, should we lower the bodies into the ground?" A soldier asked.

Umar swayed slightly on his feet, but he didn't answer.

"My prince?"

Finally, Prince Umar lifted his head. The grief that his men felt was magnified a thousand times on his face.

"Yes, lower them down," he said quietly, "But we shall pray for their souls in the after-life."

"My prince, you should not blame yourself for this," the soldier said. "How would anyone know that a menace like Saint Lawrence or his creatures would come?"

Prince Duncan strode to Prince Umar's side, clapping his shoulder with a meaty hand. "My prince, you should not give up on what your O-Father wanted," he said. "We should make plans and keep pushing."

King Duncan looked right into Umar's eyes, which were full of despair.

"How can I not blame myself?" Umar said. "I could not keep my kin safe. I couldn't even save my own brothers. Only God knows where they are now, and what the false saint might do to them." He swallowed hard, and tears shimmered in his eyes. His voice deepened with sorrow.

"I agree with you, my sumuu," he said, "But do we have the power to fight back against the false saint? The beast that he controls—how can we fight such a creature?"

The Golden Soldiers near Umar heard his cry of despair, and it touched their hearts and minds deeply. These young boys, who had trained and learned for years in the north, had always lived in peace and continuous light. Now they watched as the dead bodies of their kin were lowered into early graves, drained of light and hope. The hearts of the living were also lowered, dropping into a gray, dark world of despair.

"These bodies will lay here until the end of time," Umar whispered. "I was unable to help my kin back home. They will always lie here, in this forgotten place."

He stood silently while mud was shoveled across their bodies.

"My prince, the soldiers are buried," a soldier near him finally said. "May God grant them peace."

Umar, shocked out of his grief-stricken reverie, glanced up. His fellow kin who still lived now seemed to feel as hopeless as he did. He walked past the unmarked graves and turned to his soldiers, who stared at the graves as if they lived in a nightmare.

"I remember being young, running wild around the Tower of Light," Umar said softly. "The snow was always falling there, but it never touched the ground. Sometimes it got close, though. On those days, my brothers and I would stick out our tongues to try to catch the snow. We always wanted to taste it, but we never could. It melted before it could touch our tongues."

He cleared his throat and spoke louder, pulling his shoulders back.

"I remember one night, when the wind was strong and the snow was falling fast," he said. "I asked a few of you to come out and help us catch the snowflakes that fell, so we could taste it. It was a stupid thing to do, and I felt foolish even trying it, but we still tried.

"That night, we succeeded," he said. "Do you remember this? We caught it, and we regretted it. The snow was salty and it had a strong, unpleasant taste, but we finished that task anyway."

Now Umar held his head high, and his white eyes began to blaze with passion. "I did not lead this cavalry so we could go to an early death," he said. "I led this cavalry because you are my friends. You are the same friends who helped me catch and taste snow. You are the friends I promised to protect, and you are the friends that I now call upon to fellowship with me again in trust."

Now the blaze in his eyes became an inferno, but it wasn't the same bright light the soldiers had seen in his eyes in the northern lands. Everything he said now was tainted with the idea of revenge.

"We'll avenge the deaths of our kin!" he shouted. "We'll bring justice to the Saint for what has happened this week. I promise you this, and I promise myself this. We will bring that false saint to justice or death. My friends, will you help me again? Will you follow me? My friends, will you trust me again?" Umar marched up and down the line, looking into the eyes of his kin to show them that he could still lead them in the face of darkness and fear.

King Duncan and Prince Sumer looked at each other. "He's as headstrong as his father," Duncan said.

King Duncan kept an eye on Prince Umar for the rest of the day, watching his face as it turned from sorrow and grief to anger and back again. By the time the heavy night rains set in, he had a plan that he felt he could present to the young ruler.

"Do not worry about your brothers, my prince," King Duncan said. "I'll march south, down to the Royal Castle of Nicaea. This place is ruled by councilmen. Maybe I can persuade them to fight on your side, before we make any solid plans to attack the false saint."

"Will that be enough men?" Prince Umar raised his head, searching King Duncan's face.

"It will be if you bring the honorable knights from the West-lands," King Duncan said. "If you can gather them, we'll surely have a chance to save your brothers."

"Who are these people from the Royal Castle of Nicaea?" Umar asked, and something dark flared in his eyes. "Why would they aid us?"

"The Nicaea people are Norms from the Middle-lands," King Duncan said. "Just as our kin went north, some went south to the Castle of Nicaea, where they were taken in and saved from the massive slaughter that took place here."

Prince Umar looked doubtful. He looked away, but King Duncan called his attention again.

"Trust me, my prince," he said. "They will aid us if we ask them to."

Umar stood and paced through the tent, deep in thought. The choices were at such odds with each other. He wanted to march south immediately to find his brothers who had been taken, but King Duncan's words made sense.

Prince Sumer, who had been listening silently, cleared his throat.

"Your highness," he said in a soft voice, "I have no plans to head west or south. My people do not fare well in these environments, so rather than venture further, we shall stay here and protect the people of Mik-Mag."

Sumer was surprised when Prince Umar smiled. He walked over and placed a hand on Sumer's shoulder.

"Thank you, Sumer," he said. "Your choice is your own, but these Norms do need help and protection. Your kin are quick and wise, so they will be a great help, but heed my warning. These Norms do not like outsiders. They may be even less receptive of Qazams than they were of my Golden Soldiers."

"I understand," Sumer said. "We'll keep our distance from the Mik-Mag people, but if you ever need us, my prince, we'll surely come to your aid." He stood and began to bow before Prince Umar.

"No," Umar said, grabbing Sumer's shoulders. "Do not bow. After much thinking, I've decided to retract from my title as prince, and from any title related to the royal family."

"What?" King Duncan almost yelled.

"I won't answer to a high title until I can make things right again," Umar said. "I wonder what my O-Father would think of me, when I have allowed so much blood to be shed here. The men and beasts I slaughtered fell to my sword in a brutal, gruesome way, and then I lost my brothers. I'll only regain my title if I return my brothers safe and sound to my O-Father. May he forgive me for my failures."

His voice trailed off uncertainly and King Duncan stood. As the eldest fighter in this dark place, he was the most like a father-figure to these boys. He understood how the rain and the darkness must feel to them, and he felt a deep need to reassure them. He walked around the table to stand next to them.

"I respect both of your decisions, but we can and should move out of this area," he said. "If other soldiers hear about this battle, they'll surely come and try to claim anything that's left for themselves and the people here will suffer more."

"What soldiers?" Sumer asked.

"Soldiers such as Janissaries, or even worse, Marid rebels," King Duncan said. "Umar, trust me. I know the pain of loss. We lose so much in these forgotten lands, even our memories of our families. My mother was here when the soldiers from the south and unknown lands in the east marched here. They slaughtered all the children and babies. Without a thought, they chained those who tried to run, and they chased down all those who were able to flee."

He took a deep breath, blinking at the depth of emotion that had risen in his heart. When he spoke again, his voice rasped deeply.

"Those soldiers are called the Asward soldiers," King Duncan said. "They roam these lands and kill all who oppose their rule. Trust me, Umar, you got lucky. Many of your men died, but some of your kin still live. If we had not come, those Asward soldiers and the Ragrok beast would have slain you all, as well as the rest of the Norms that live in this city."

Umar was shocked to his core. He looked at King Duncan as if he had never seen him before. His own family knew such horror, such hopelessness, and still he had become such an honorable man.

"You speak truthfully, King Duncan," Umar said. "Please accept my apologies for your kin and for what has happened here to the city of Mik-Mag. We are surely on the right side. We must fight back those who bring harm, just like those who died during the Golden Age, but with such odds, how can we fight back? How can we move against such a powerful enemy?"

CHAPTER THIRTY-ONE – So It Begins

As the doubt deepened in Umar's heart, the darkness grew stronger throughout the land of Amer. It infected the inhabitants with a curse that spread from an unknown place—or, perhaps, a person.

Thus far, the darkness had not spread into the North. A handful of people could feel it creeping, coming ever nearer.

Deep in the Qazam woods, inside their cave, the candle-maidens sat silently. For days after King Alm's visit, they did nothing but sit, staring into the single candle that illuminated the cave.

One afternoon, as the candle burned low, a candle-maiden made an odd noise.

"Ahh," she said, as she fell dead onto the table. The other two candle-maidens did not move.

Marta knew the sign. She smiled slightly.

"So," she said, "The oath-keeper made it to the Jinn."

As the other remaining candle-maiden nodded, Marta stood, walked to the entrance of the cave, and looked out on the forested world around her.

"And so, it begins," she said in a soft voice.

PEOPLE AND PLACES

Those Who Fight for the Light

High King Alm – The King of the North. King Alm was a king from ages ago, and living in the tower of light has extended his life and the lives of his kin. Unfortunately, the age of darkness has tainted the High King's heart.

Amir – King Alm's magical pet lion. Amir, who was found by Alm's father, Ashhad, near the High King woods, is one of the biggest lions in the land of Amer. He is also the only one with speech powers and the ability to transport from one location to another.

King Idun – King of the Qazam. Many do not know where the Qazam came from, but they live in peace beyond the High King's road. King Idun lives in grief over the loss of his eldest son during the battles of the Golden Age.

Queen Meltôriel – Queen of the Qazam and wife of Idun. Meltôriel's voice is known to have beauty and the power of persuasion.

King Duncan – King of the northern Norms, and the son of the boy who spoke to High King Alm about the growing darkness during the Golden Age.

Nimra – A Qazam girl who lives with her grandmother, Marta, because her father was murdered and her mother went missing.

Ismail – The oath-keeper and youngest son of High King Alm

Laenatan - a young boy from the Golden Age who was cursed and transformed by the candle-maidens until he is finally able to complete his oath

Aikiba – Aikiba is a knight from the West Kingdom who was lost in the Widow Woods and then found by Ismail and Nimra. Aikiba is tall and has the strength to single-handedly wield a great-sword.

Umar – The eldest of King Alm's sons, who leads the golden armies south to Mik-Mag.

Kaf – A son of High King Alm

Adn – A son of High King Alm

Sumer – The second son of King Idun and Queen Meltôriel, who leads the Qazam army

Zubair – High King Alm's right hand and father to Zuda.

Zuda – Zuda is a good friend to Kaf, and like Kaf, he trained with King Alm's brother near the High King's Forest.

Blaize – A blacksmith from the northern Norm tribe. Blaize is an unmarried Norm who was tasked to teach the young Norms to learn the trade of blacksmithing and building homes, walls, wells and caves.

Marta – Marta is one of the three remaining candle-maidens, whose tasks are unknown but manifold.

Azui – The youngest soldier in the Golden Army. Azui is just a few years older than Ismail himself, and even looks like Ismail, except he has blue eyes rather than white.

Sarvajna - Sarvajna is a young monk and the last of his kind. He lived in the High King's woods.

Mehreen – A woman from the Castle of Blayney, who is jailed along with other mothers of the boys who were hanged in the castle.

Old King Hazens - A figure who has been heard of as the mad king who rules the far West-lands.

Those Who Fight for the Dark

Ibies – The Cursed One

Saint Lawrence – Youngest of the Oligarchs, always learning and finding ways to get more power. Saint Lawrence was orphan from the great city of Minar.

Ingie - The leader of the troops and captain of the jailers at the Tower of Hasiphane, which is ruled by Saint Lawrence.

Hassen – A spy from KHAD group, Hassen would really rather earn quick coins rather than be a real spy.

Jailers – Men who work under Ingie's command to torture captured prisoners and elicit information. They wear masks and carry torches.

 Cassini – A son of an elder from the city of Mik-Mag, who has power from his father's rank, but also always has darkness in him. Some believe he aspires to become an Oligarch.

Asward Soldiers – Under the command of Saint Lawrence, these men ride into battle on the backs of enormous spiders taken from the Widow Woods.

Spiders – Evil creatures from the Widow Woods who covet gold and gems.

Sieg – The spider trainer and head Asward soldier, who serves under Saint Lawrence.

Oligarchs - Corrupt Leaders who spread Ibies' evil throughout the lands. Not much is known about the except that they are all Norms who have had a taste of power.

Vicar – One of the most brutal Oligarchs, the Vicar lives in the west, close to the Golden Gates and the Widow Woods.

Valerian - Captain of the soldiers who serve under the Vicar, and also captain of the Cipher.

Igor – A spider from the Widow Woods

Sultan -A scholar from the Castle of Blayney

Cipher – A shadow-like mist that lures victims by appearing to be what they desire most to see

KHAD – a spy group that infiltrates most of the lands and only reports to Ibies

Ragrok – A snake-like creatures that slides on the ground. The Ragrok has a long neck, big red eyes, razor-sharp fangs and deadly venom.

Ubir – brown-skinned animals with long fur. Ubir suck the blood from dead bodies and will fight amongst themselves for a fresh body.

Locations

The Land of Amer – This land was created thousands of years ago. Some creatures from the first ages still live here, but they are few in numbers, and they hide in white trees or underground. Others are locked away...far away.

Tower of Light – The Tower of Light is a large structure from which a mysterious light emanates. Its power is felt by all who live in the north-lands.

High King's Forest – The High King's Forest is home to many of the old creatures who lived in the land before the Norms, Qazams and Northern Kin arrived.

Haeinsa – The tower of the monks, deep in the High King's Forest, where the few remaining monks live and wait to set the oath-keeper on his journey.

City of Mik-Mag – The City of Mik-Mag used to be a big market of trade. At the end of the Golden Age, it was attacked and burnt beyond any hope of repair. The people who still inhabit the area live in constant fear and despair.

Widow Woods – The woods close to the north-west side of the Golden Gates, where spiders the size of horses live.

Qazam Forest - Far beyond the High King's road live the Qazams, a race of elves that love trees. The Qazams are ruled by King Idun.

Tower of Hasiphane - Also known as the Slaughterhouse, the Tower of Hasiphane is ruled by Saint Lawrence.

Coven Cave – Coven Cave is where the candle-maidens live, deep in the Qazam Forest.

The Royal Castle of Nicaea – In the lands south of Mik-Mag, the castle is ruled by the Council of Nicaea.

Wildlife

Pigs, crows, Horse, Lions, demon dogs, ciphers, dogs, cats, Ragrok beasts, bears, cattle, goats, Markhor, Marsh, Sand Cat, Blackbuck, Roc, Falak, and Nasnas.

ABOUT THE AUTHOR

Marhaba, I'm Nauman Raja, and I'm the author of "The Land of Amer." This is my first book.

I was born in a small village in Pakistan. Ever since we moved to Pennsylvania, I was always interested in fantasy books, but my reading skills were limited. Many times, I ended up creating my own story out of the stories I was trying to read. I found this easier for me when I was growing up and learning, but my love for fantasy evolved into a desire to create it myself.

I discovered that I wanted to write a high fantasy book with South Asian themes and lore and a mixture of European touches. Words, locations and names in "The Land of Amer" are all based in a South Asian background. I hope readers enjoy and piece together the story, as I used to do when reading as a child.

I invite you to discover The Land of Amer on Twitter. Please follow **@land_Amer** and keep the conversation about this series going!

Made in the USA
Monee, IL
06 March 2020

22826686R00116